"Come on. Let's get out of here."

The quad spun around next to her, kicking dust in the air. Norwood extended his hand.

The half smile floating over those oh-so-perfect lips gave her the reassuring charge of energy she needed. She gripped his hand. He pulled her up and she climbed onto the back.

"Hang on tight. It's going to get bumpy."

Norwood gave the quad gas. Dirt and gravel spun out behind the big wheels as he headed toward the road. Drina had to loosen her hold slightly, but not too much, as they hit bumps. Even though she and Norwood were almost strangers and he might be a traitor to their country, his strong, sturdy body seemed the only solid, stable thing in an exploding world. She clung to him with all her might.

The ATV reached the dirt road leading back to town. They dipped down into the culvert and started to climb the other side. Drina glanced back at the shed and the pile of equipment behind it. Still no sign of Carter. They were safe, really safe.

But for how long?

Tanya Stowe is a Christian fiction author with an unexpected edge. She is married to the love of her life, her high school sweetheart. They have four children and twenty-one grandchildren, a true adventure. She fills her books with the unusual—mysteries and exotic travel, even a murder or two. No matter where Tanya takes you—on a trip to foreign lands or a suspenseful journey packed with danger—be prepared for the extraordinary.

Books by Tanya Stowe

Love Inspired Suspense

Mojave Rescue

MOJAVE RESCUE

TANYA STOWE

HARLEQUIN® LOVE INSPIRED® SUSPENSE

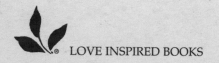

LOVE INSPIRED BOOKS

ISBN-13: 978-1-335-54354-7

Mojave Rescue

www.Harlequin.com

Printed in U.S.A.

Trust in the Lord with all thine heart;
and lean not unto thine own understanding. In all
thy ways acknowledge Him, and He shall direct thy paths.
—Proverbs 3:5-6

For Delia Latham because this and many other books would not be possible without you. Thank you, my friend.

ONE

"Bill, I did it!" Drina Gallagher almost dropped her cell phone in her excitement.

"Did what?" Bill Carlisle's sleepy voice rolled across her senses, setting off a faint thread of regret for waking her boss in the middle of the night. Excitement quickly overrode the flash of remorse.

"I did it, Bill. I fixed the problem."

"Drina? Do you have any idea what time it is?"

She didn't. Secluded in a small office at the desert test facility, her focus had been completely fixed on the data that had turned up in today's field test. Not only had she lost track of time, but Drina was at Edwards Air Force Base on the West Coast for the test. Bill was at the company headquarters on the East Coast...where it was three in the morning.

"I'm sorry. I forgot the time again. But I knew you'd want to hear this now."

"Wait...did you say *problem*? Is there a problem with the program?"

"No...well, yes, there was. I set up today's work based on the parameters you and I discussed yesterday and everything went haywire. The numbers didn't make sense."

Drina's company had been awarded a military contract to develop a nonlethal energy-directed weapon that would protect soldiers against supersonic missiles and unmanned aerial vehicles. Their energy-directed weapon needed to impact machines only, destroying the electronics of missiles and UAVs, rendering them useless against ground troops. But the weapon needed to be rechargeable to full power in a short time and, above all, small enough for transport on a ground vehicle. So far, Drina and her company had failed to meet those parameters.

Until today. Today faulty tests led Drina to an epiphany. The answer came to her in an amazing eye-opening moment, followed by hours of furious number crunching that proved her theory possible.

"The numbers from the test were off so I created an equation using new figures and...it worked. I solved the problem." Drina repeated the news for the third time, just to hear the words out loud again.

Succeeding meant everything to her. Creating a nonlethal energy-directed weapon would secure her company's position and create jobs. It would solidify Drina's place in her parents' exclusive scientific community, but most important, it would fulfill her deepest desire to protect American soldiers. Riddled by guilt, Drina was determined to create a weapon that would help protect America's military personnel.

No one knew the secret that pushed Drina to work long hours, to forget to eat and sometimes even to sleep. Not even Bill, the mentor who had hired her straight out of MIT four years ago, knew what drove her. It was her secret alone to nurse, obsess about and feel guilt over.

Sometimes Drina wondered if even God knew.

"Bill, I reworked the equation five different ways and it worked every time. We'll be able to recharge the weapon to full power in less than three minutes."

"Full power?" For the first time, Bill's voice sounded awake and alert.

"Full. Power. And I think we'll be able to reduce the weight. We might even be able to go small enough for it to be carried on a soldier's back. We just need—"

"Stop, Drina! Don't say another word. This is my home phone. It's not a secure line."

Drina's breath caught in her throat. As an electronic warfare engineer, she thought in numbers, not words. Most of the constant security hype sounded like Hollywood fiction to her and she paid little heed. No matter how hard Bill tried, his emphasis on protocol and top secret measures usually went right over her head.

But not tonight. Tonight his words sent a wave of cold washing through her.

Perhaps the recent briefing by the base's head of security had impacted her more than she'd realized. He'd definitely made an impression, but it was more along the lines of his all-American good looks.

Tall, dark hair, more handsome than he had a right to be. Blue-gray eyes. Even a cute little dimple when he smiled. He had those strong, masculine, next-door-neighbor looks that most women Drina's age called cheesy but secretly adored. The kind of look that said, "Let me take care of you. I can carry the weight of the world."

Drina might have fallen for that look years ago. In fact, she did fall for it. John had that same aura about him. Now he was dead and

Drina was saddled with guilt. She wouldn't forget that lesson.

No one was that capable, and movies were just moving pictures with pretty people. Cal Norwood *could* have walked straight out of one of those Hollywood plots Drina abhorred. That was probably why she hadn't paid much attention to his talk about eyes and ears everywhere. Now she wished she'd listened.

Even as her breath caught in her throat, a click echoed over her connection with Bill. Someone else was listening on their line.

Yep. Definitely should have paid attention.

"Drina…" Bill's voice was low and taut. "Where are you? No. Don't answer. Don't give that info out over the line."

Her stomach flip-flopped.

"Where is your work?" Bill's tone was as tense as Drina felt.

"Most of it's on my computer."

"All right. You know the protocols. Email it to me using our secure server then contact Norwood. He'll know what to do."

"Okay."

Bill hung up. Drina heard the distinct double click of another line disconnecting from his landline. Someone *had* been listening.

Everything around her was dark except for the single light spilling onto her desk. All the other workers had left hours ago. She was alone, miles away from the main base in a secluded section of the rocket site.

Drina's heart threatened to pound out of her chest. But she couldn't move. Couldn't lower the phone from her ear.

Protocols. Bill said follow the protocols. She dropped her cell phone. Scratch sheets of equations covered the top of her desk. She scooped them into her arms and fed them twenty at a time into the shredder. The teeth jammed on the thick pile. Drina had to pull it loose and start again, running only ten at a time through the machine.

All the while, a small part of Norwood's two-hour lecture on security flashed through her mind. She didn't know why she remembered that particular portion word for word, but the memory of his firm, modulated voice kept her on task and calm.

Be mindful of those around you. Janitors. Cooks in the lunch cafeteria. Your coworker in the next cubicle. Eyes and ears are all around us. You never know who might be listening, gathering information.

The last of the scratch paper disappeared into the shredder. Drina sighed with relief. Grabbing her laptop, she saved the file with her own personal code, then linked with her company's secure internet connection.

Linking took precious seconds. Drina's fingers drummed on the desk with increasing rapidity. Finally, the site came up. She keyed in her password, attached the file and was about to hit Send when more of Norwood's words came back to her.

We believe the project has been compromised. We're certain someone in the network has been leaking information, so we're cautioning all of you to be extra careful.

Extra careful. A leak in the network.

Someone within her company could be giving away information. Drina shuddered. If her equations were correct and they slipped into the wrong hands, a weapon of phenomenal force could be developed. A pulse of that magnitude used on men instead of machines could destroy hearing and vision, not to mention what it might do to a human heart. Finger poised over the send button, Drina held her breath.

She would not—could not—let her work fall into the wrong hands. Thousands of lives would be lost and Drina had made it her life's goal to save lives. It was the least she could do to atone for the death for which she felt responsible.

But could she trust her own network? Was the breach here, with someone on the base or within her own company?

Drina didn't know. Couldn't know. But someone did. Grabbing her cell phone, she looked up the number Norwood had given her in the briefing and dialed. The phone rang and rang. Finally, Norwood's clear, strong voice came over the line.

"You've reached Cal Norwood. Leave a message and I'll get back to you."

Drina squeezed her eyes shut. Of course. It was past midnight. Like all normal human beings, the man was in bed…asleep. She didn't want to repeat the mistake she made with Bill by revealing info over the phone so she left a message for Norwood to call her, then hung up.

She looked around at the shadows just beyond the feeble desk lamp. They felt almost alive, lurking, watching.

No way was she waiting for Norwood to call back. Deleting the email to Bill, she saved the attached file with a pass code and shut down her laptop. After grabbing her jacket off the back of the chair, she slid the laptop into her backpack, pulled out her keys and headed for the door of the small office.

The desk light stayed on. She couldn't face

the dark right now. Outside the small office, a long, empty corridor led to the front. That stretch of blackness would be more than enough to cross.

She opened the door and stood in the portal, light pouring into the black hall, and stared down the long, inky stretch of about forty feet. The main doors were just around the corner. Still, the corridor seemed endless.

She fumbled in her jacket pocket for her cell phone, grateful it had a flashlight app. Just as she swiped her phone menu up, the desk lamp behind her switched off. Sudden darkness blanketed the room, and she heard the slow whirring of machines shutting down.

The power had been cut off.

Fingers trembling, she fumbled with her cell phone. She needed light. Now.

The main door clicked open. The soft tread of someone walking down the hall echoed in the Stygian darkness.

The light on her cell phone flashed on, illuminating the corridor like a spotlight. Drina pressed the off button, stuffed the phone in her pocket, turned and ran in the opposite direction.

Even with her heart pounding in her ears she could hear her tennis shoes squeaking on the linoleum floor. Whoever was behind her surely heard her clamoring down the hall. An emergency exit waited just around the corner. If she could get out the door and around the building, she might reach her car ahead of whoever was behind her. She'd lock the doors and speed straight to the closest military police station.

The red exit sign above the door was a welcoming beacon. She raced to it, slammed into the security bar and skidded out onto the raised entrance.

A blast of cold Mojave Desert wind slapped at her face, nearly robbing her of breath. Drina had only been to this test facility a few times but she'd already developed an intense dislike of the wind. Its cold touch made her shiver even more. Thankfully, she'd cut her dark hair into a short bob just before coming here. No long strands blocked her view as she gripped the handrail with both hands and slid under. She landed on her feet and took off at a run even before she had her balance.

She stumbled and almost fell, only stopping herself by pushing against the side of the building. Arms pumping, she ran toward the front, fearful she might trip again without moonlight to guide her. But she dared not slow down.

Reaching the corner of the building, she

came to a skidding halt. A man in dark clothing stood near her car, the lone vehicle in the parking lot. Was that a gun in his hand? Drina caught her breath and held it, not daring to make a sound. Her gaze darted to the side.

Joshua trees with their unique thick branches and straggly coatings marked the edge of the hill and were silhouetted against the night sky. The road back to the main portion of the rocket site looped around this building on the hilltop. The paved road was just below the trees. If she could get down the hill without tumbling and hurting herself, she could follow the road back to the cluster of buildings and find help.

Drina spun back around and banged hard against the bulky form of another man dressed in all dark clothing. She would have fallen to the ground if he hadn't grasped her, clutching her to his chest with one arm. He loomed over her, a faceless silhouette, and held on tight as she silently struggled to break free. The stars overhead outlined his raised fist…just before it crashed against the side of her jaw and everything went black.

Cal Norwood pushed the visor of his car up as he reached the shadows of the mountains. Edwards Air Force Base was located on the far eastern edge of a three-sided valley that spilled into the vast Mojave Desert. He'd been driving west, straight into the setting sun for forty minutes. From the moment he'd locked his office door on the base and headed to the meeting place, his senses had snapped like broken electric wires.

He eased off the asphalt to the dirt service road and slowed to a halt. Gripping the steering wheel, he scanned the countryside for a car then the air for a helicopter…anything that would give him a hint of what waited for him just over the hill.

Nothing. Not a sign, nor a sound. Not even tire tracks of the car he knew was there.

Please, Lord. Don't let it be true. Don't let her be in that shack. I won't give up…not now when I'm so close. Buddy deserves justice.

Earlier this morning he'd listened to Drina Gallagher's message and was filled with dread. He'd dressed and rushed to the complex, only to find her empty rented car in the parking lot, signs of a struggle in the dirt and her car keys on the ground. He believed her disappearance had something to do with the text he'd received the evening before from his secret contact.

You got your wish. Be at the shack at 5 p.m. tomorrow. You're meeting the boss.

Two years ago Cal's best friend died at the hands of a black market gang. Andrew Sterling, Buddy to his friends, had been Cal's friend most of their lives. They grew up in a quaint older housing tract perched on the hills of San Diego, overlooking the bay. Together they'd watched the big navy ships sail in and out and promised each other that one day, they'd do their part. Buddy had joined the NCIS. Cal had joined the CIA.

After Buddy was killed, the Department of Defense and the CIA created a joint task force to infiltrate and uncover the gang stealing weapon plans from all the military forces. Cal called in a few favors and wrangled an undercover position on the force. His assignment had turned into two long years of leaks, dead ends and betrayals. Driven, he was determined one way or another to stop these men from killing more people. He ate, slept and lived for the moment when he could finally bring the gang down and serve up justice for Buddy and countless others.

Then last night the text had come through. He was finally going to meet the devious leader of a group who had infiltrated the highest echelons of government security and still managed to escape detection. The end was so close Cal could taste it…until he'd heard Drina's message. The taste of victory turned sour in his mouth.

An already-dangerous situation had been made even more complicated by the disappearance of one dark-haired scientist.

Drina Gallagher was brilliant—and prettier than he'd anticipated. He'd heard so much praise about her work, he'd expected an older, more staid woman to walk into his briefing room, not a perky, petite beauty who created an immediate internal reaction he didn't want or expect.

Drina hid behind some overlarge black-rimmed spectacles, but that was where the scientist stereotype ended. Behind those glasses was a pert nose, a pair of hazel-colored eyes that seemed to change color with her mood and a tiny, fragile-looking body. Capped by a head of short, shiny black hair that wanted to curl, she looked more like a hyperbubbly nerd than a world-renowned scientist…a nerd that had somehow ignited feelings Cal had buried deep with his true identity.

She sparked sweet thoughts of laughter and fun, which was ridiculous because her out-of-sync look hid a snarky attitude. Some of the men on his team in Washington believed she might be the spy. But Cal had recognized her I'm-checking-out look as soon as he began his briefing on security. Drina Gallagher wasn't the leak. She was just as driven as he. Focused on her work and nothing else. He doubted she'd heard a word of his briefing or even cared about being cautious.

Maybe if she'd paid attention she wouldn't be missing right now, and two long, desperate years of Cal's work wouldn't be on the line.

As he'd alerted her superiors and his, he wondered if the man behind the text was "the boss." Was his contact the mastermind who had eluded detection for so long? Was Cal being played...and lured into a trap?

He didn't know the answers and until he did, until he met and could identify the traitor, he couldn't take any chances or trust anyone—not the military, not Drina's company, not even the security detail he worked with on the base. What was more, he couldn't shake the feeling that there was a direct link between his scheduled meeting with the boss and Drina Gallagher's disappearance.

During the long day his on-base security team had contacted Drina's coworkers and family, searching for a reason she might have chosen to disappear. They dusted for finger-prints—even tried to match shoe patterns in the dirt beside the place where Drina's keys were found. They found no evidence, no clues as to who might have snatched her. That fact alone convinced Cal that the boss and his gang were involved. They never made mistakes and Cal's team had no idea what had happened to the petite engineer.

But Cal had a sinking feeling in his gut. The text about his meeting with the boss had come too close to Drina's kidnapping to be a coincidence. It felt more like a step-by-step process…like they were leading Cal to something.

All day long his mind went over scenarios and possibilities—some path, any avenue he could take to salvage his undercover identity and still save the girl because there was no doubt in his mind she was in that shack. Once he drove over that hill, both their lives would be in deadly danger.

Whir. Whir. Whir.

The soft spinning sound matched the throbbing in Drina's cheek. She opened her eyes bit by bit, hoping to pinpoint the source of the noise. Instead, everything began to spin so badly, she thought she might throw up. She gagged and, for the first time, felt the tape across her mouth.

Panic surged through her. She tried to reach for the tape but her hands were tied at her back. The sharp plastic edge of a zip tie cut into her wrists.

Panic swept over her and her gag reflex kicked in again.

Calm down, Drina! Close your eyes. Breathe slow and deep.

Inhaling through her nose eased the roiling in her stomach. Slowly but surely, she calmed her breathing. Awareness returned. She lay on the ground, on her side. Dirty grit bit into her cheek. The soft whirring remained in the background—steady, consistent, like the beat of a drum or…a wind turbine.

Giant wind turbines dotted the hills surrounding the mountain passes into the valley. Those turbines turned the ever-present gusts coming through the passes into energy. Drina had taken a tour of one of the wind farms on her first trip out west. Now she recognized the sound of the massive blades swooping through the air.

She braced herself, then opened her eyes bit by bit. Vertigo didn't overwhelm her this time but it took a moment to focus. She lay facing a door. Sunlight streamed in beneath it. She wasn't on the ground after all, but on a rough-textured slab of cement. Wind gusted and the metal walls and roof rattled. Shovels and picks hanging along the wall began a precarious shimmy that threatened to send them tumbling to the floor.

She had to be in one of the small service shacks beneath the turbine fields. She wasn't sure where, but she knew the base had no tall turbines that would interfere with air traffic. The base and any kind of military police or help was far, far away.

What time was it? How long had she been unconscious? Where were the men who'd kidnapped her?

My backpack. Where's my backpack?

She rolled over, her gaze scouring the shed. Her backpack and computer were nowhere to be seen. She sagged against the floor. Those men, whoever they were, had all her information. Had they fled and left her here? How long would it be before someone found her stranded in this little-used shed? Or, worse yet, would her captors return?

A thousand questions marched through Drina's mind…all soundless…all unanswered. She lay for what seemed like hours until the steady pounding in the side of her head faded and she drifted back to sleep.

She woke to the sound of a car. Instantly, Drina tensed. Could it be the service people… or had her captors returned?

Her gaze darted to the door. The sunlight beneath was dimmer; it was later in the day.

The car stopped. Doors opened. Gravel crunched as someone stepped out.

"He's late."

Drina didn't recognize the voice, but it sent a shiver up her spine. Deep, hard…and cold as arctic ice.

"What do you expect?" Another voice. "With the girl missing, the base is on high alert. They've had him on the spot all day."

The man they were waiting for was someone who worked at the base? Could he be the leak Norwood had talked about?

"All I can say is, it's about time he earned his pay." The first man spoke again, his voice tinged with disgust. "Frankly, I don't think he's worth the money the boss pays him."

"Not our business, Whitson. Besides, the inside info he's passed on has helped."

Drina caught her breath. The man they waited for *was* the informant.

"It better help. I'm getting itchy and when I'm itchy, trouble's on the way. I want to get out of here before it hits."

"Relax. The boss knows what he's doing."

"I'm not so sure. Not this time. I'm telling you, Carter, kidnapping that girl was a mistake."

"You won't say that after the boss sells that weapon of hers. It's gonna give you a nice tidy fortune."

These men were black market munitions sellers. They'd offer her plans to the highest bidder. Sagging against the gritty floor, she trembled. Everything she feared was coming to pass and she could do nothing to stop it.

"There's his car."

Drina listened, every muscle in her body tense. Another car engine came closer and stopped. A door opened, setting off a loud beep, clearly audible inside the shed. Given its persistence, the driver must have left the door open and the keys in the ignition.

"About time you got here. The helicopter is on its way." Whitson spoke first. Drina barely heard his growled words over the insistent chirp of the alarm.

"It can't land here with all these wind turbines." The annoying alarm made it hard to hear, but she knew that voice from somewhere…

"Our rendezvous point is just over the hill in an open space." Carter sounded calm.

"Yeah, and you almost missed it." Whitson

butted in. He seemed determined to take his frustration out on the newcomer.

"What did you expect? You left me with a mess. I had eyes and ears all around me."

Eyes and ears. The words and the voice coalesced. Drina knew where she'd heard both, and her blood turned cold.

Cal Norwood, head of program security. The man she was supposed to trust had betrayed her.

Panic assaulted her senses. Her breath came in rapid gulps. Nausea rose again. But Norwood's next words stopped the rising fear like a brick wall.

"What happened to the girl?"

"She's in the shed."

"Here? You brought her here? What were you thinking?"

Even Drina could hear the threat in his tone.

"Relax, Norwood. The boss ordered it. Did you bring the money?"

"Yeah, but I don't like it. Twenty thousand dollars is a lot of money just to be carrying around."

"Don't worry. You'll get it back. And then some. Hand it over."

Their actions came to Drina like muddled

rustlings. She had no idea what was going on. Until Norwood spoke again.

"That's the girl's backpack."

"Yep. We're going to put the money in her bag and leave it behind."

A long pause followed. "You want to make it look like she sold us the plans."

"Finally, the bright boy catches on." Drina was beginning to hate Whitson's nasty attitude.

"We need suspicion thrown off you." Carter's tone acted like a balm on the tension between Norwood and Whitson. "We'll leave your car here, door open, keys in. Eventually the gas will run out and it'll look like you stumbled onto our exchange, caught us in the act and the girl got hurt in the resulting conflict."

"You mean killed."

Norwood's words made Drina's blood drain.

"What's the matter? Squeamish now that the real work's starting?"

Whitson seemed determined to start a fight with Norwood. But the traitor kept his cool, not responding to the other man's insulting baits.

"Shut up, Whitson." Carter took the lead. Drina heard a thud of something tossed.

"Plant the money and finish this. I'll check with the guys in the helicopter to see how far out they are."

Finish this. *He means finish me.*

Desperate, Drina rolled to her back again. Her gaze swept the shed for an escape or a weapon…something. Maybe if she could get to that shovel…

The door opened before she could move. Norwood filled the portal. He looked taller. Still handsome in his black leather jacket and jeans. Like a dark messenger bringing death.

He held her backpack in his hands. Crossing the room, he knelt and laid it beside her. He was close enough for her to see the gray tint of his blue eyes and the taut tension lines along the side of his mouth. Suddenly, he winked.

Drina's eyes widened. What in the world…?

"Open the backpack and pull some of the money out on the floor." Whitson had followed Norwood in. "Make it look like we had a fight."

The man looked the way he sounded. Short. Shaved head. Solid…like a bodybuilder. And he had a gun clamped in one meaty fist.

"Here's the deal, Norwood. We can't make it look like she's the guilty party unless we shed just a little of your blood, too. So I'm gonna have to break your nose. You can imagine how unhappy that makes me." The man's grin radiated pure evil.

Drina's gaze darted back to Norwood's. He raised his eyebrows as if to say, "Ready?"

Ready for what?

Barely moving, his hand shifted ever so slightly beneath his jacket. Drina followed the movement and saw a gun tucked into his waistband. His finger flicked a lock.

Drina looked up, startled. He was going to shoot Whitson while she lay trussed up, helpless and in the direct line of fire.

Drina started to protest, to shake her head. Norwood raised his eyebrows again and nodded a signaled countdown. Once… Twice…

No, I'm not ready!

Her screamed protest was muffled by the tape and didn't stop Norwood's countdown. When he reached three, he rolled to his side, pulled the gun loose and fired.

TWO

Whitson's face slacked in shock before he doubled over. His fingers clinched on the trigger and bullets ripped across the shed. Norwood dived for Drina, covering her body with his.

The gunfire stopped. Leaping to his feet, Norwood kicked the gun away from Whitson's body. Then he pulled a knife out of his pocket and knelt beside Drina.

"We only have seconds." He cut the zip tie at her feet. "We need to get to my car."

He cut the tie at her hands and pulled the tape loose from her mouth. Drina took a much-needed breath and tried to speak but the fire burning through her hands and feet cut her words short. All she could do was cry out.

"I know. The circulation hurts like crazy, but you've got to stand up."

Norwood pulled her to her feet and held her

upright as her legs and ankles screamed and refused to work. He hooked his arm around her waist and dragged her across the shed to peek out.

"It looks clear. Let's go."

Pulling her behind him, Norwood stepped outside. Drina followed. A bullet hit the doorway near her head, piercing the metal edge with a jagged hole. This time her scream echoed loud and clear. Norwood fired back, pointing in the direction of the black SUV parked in front.

With one swift move, Norwood pulled her away from the door and around the corner of the shed. Drina barely had time to see Carter's head popping up on the other side of the vehicle. Right in front of the shooter, on the SUV's hood, was her computer. Norwood pushed her down and she sprawled to the ground while he knelt and fired back.

More bullets pierced the metal shed, going straight through to where they crouched. Norwood ducked lower.

"We can't stay here. Can you run yet?"

She nodded, hoping she could. Crawling to the back of the shed, Drina cringed as jagged rocks pierced her palms. Her rescuer pointed to an outcropping of rocks about thirty feet away.

"When I say go, run for those rocks. Don't stop and don't look back. Got it?"

She nodded.

"Go!"

Drina leaped to her feet and almost fell. Norwood grasped her arm and steadied her as they half ran, half stumbled across the open space. She expected to feel a bullet pierce her back any minute.

They spilled over the rocks. Norwood rolled. Drina fell flat, gasping, her lungs burning almost as much as her hands and feet. She lay face up, her eyes closed.

"I don't believe this. It can't be happening."

Norwood crawled back to the rock wall and peeked over. "Believe it. My worst nightmare and what you thought would never happen just happened." He took aim and fired back at the shack. "We can't stay here. Carter can keep us pinned down indefinitely...at least long enough for the helicopter to show up. Then we'll be outnumbered." His gaze shot to the culvert below. "Look down there."

Drina rose to her elbows and peered down at a small metal shed—right next to an all-terrain vehicle.

"If I can get down there, I think I can get that quad started." Norwood cast a worried glance her way. "You'll never make it down this hill, but I can come back for you."

Drina stared at him, eyes wide, nodding, punctuating each of his words with a dip of her head.

"You…will…come back for me, won't you?"

He paused, grasped her arm and squeezed. That little touch was the most reassuring thing she'd felt in twenty-four hours.

He pulled Whitson's gun out of his waistband. "Take this."

She stared at the black weapon and shook her head. "I… I can't kill anyone."

"You wouldn't hit him even if you tried. Every time you see Carter pop his head out, point and fire. He'll think it's me. That will give me time to get down there without him shooting me."

He flipped the lock and handed it to her. She grasped it with numb, tingling fingers.

"Remember, just point and click."

She nodded again, then rose enough to peek over the rock, just in time to see Carter at the corner of the shed. Norwood took the gun out of her hand, aimed and fired. Carter lunged back out of sight. Cal gripped her hand and placed the weapon back in her palm.

"Fire again every minute or so. That'll make him keep his head down. Watch the other side of the shed. He'll try to come at you from there next."

With that, he crawled to the edge of the rocks and slid down. She watched him kick dirt high in the air as he loped down the hillside three...four steps at a time, dodging around two fallen Joshua trees, straggly coated arms still reaching to the sky. Carter fired another shot, which startled Drina. Turning, she fired the gun...just to make noise. She had no idea where the bullet went, but she had to protect Cal. Maybe he was the leak, a traitor to their country. But he'd just saved her life and was helping her to escape. He deserved her help in return.

She fired again then turned back to watch Cal sprint across the clearing to the shed below. Grasping the ATV, he shook it, probably rattling the gas tank. Then he used the handle of his gun to break the lock on the plastic compartment and lifted the lid.

Carter fired another shot. It pinged off a nearby rock and forced Drina to turn around. Closing her eyes, she counted.

Numbers, she could do. Numbers were normal. They gave her courage. At sixty, she popped her head up, closed her eyes and pulled the trigger.

Dirt splayed up in the air ten feet in front of the shed.

If she kept aiming like that, Carter would know it wasn't Norwood firing. She counted again, closed one eye and tried to aim for the shed.

Carter popped his head out. She fired but lost the bullet again. No telltale spray of dirt or ping of metal indicated that she'd even come close. She absolutely had to do better or Carter would know it was her shooting. Then he'd do something crazy like charge the rocks.

She fired again and again. Carter popped his head out here and there, like he was playing cat and mouse with her, growing braver each time.

He must have realized Norwood was gone.

Somewhere in the culvert below she heard the ATV engine start up. Carter heard it, too. He stuck his head out farther than usual.

Drina took aim and actually hit the shed. Carter ducked back, but slowly…as if he knew he wasn't in any real danger of being hit.

A long time passed. Had the man moved to the other side of the shed, as Norwood had suggested?

Sure enough, Carter peeked out from the

opposite side. He looked to the left, about ten feet away at a stacked-high pile of sheet metal and damaged windmill blades. The equipment was only a few feet from the side of the hill. If he reached the shelter of that pile, it was a short distance to the edge of the cliff and a clear shot at Norwood.

Suppressing a whimper, Drina took aim and fired. All she heard was an empty click. She was out of bullets.

Carter took that moment to dash across the space to the safety of the discarded equipment.

Drina dropped the gun. Now what? How could she stop him? She heard the revving of the ATV engine again. In minutes, Norwood would be climbing up the hill…straight into Carter's line of fire.

Frantically, her gaze searched the surrounding area…and saw nothing. No weapon. No help. Nothing.

But she heard another engine.

Norwood's car was still running. Could she reach it? Carter wasn't looking her way. His attention was focused on the culvert.

Not giving herself time to think, she dashed across the open space back to the shed. Carter never even turned his head. He knew the real threat was down below with Norwood.

Gasping, her whole body tingling with adrenaline, she rounded the corner of the shed. Her gaze landed on her computer, still resting on the short hood of the SUV.

No way was she leaving that behind. She grabbed the laptop, tucked it under her arm. Halfway to the car she remembered the money. Money funded these men and their violent acts. She wouldn't leave that behind, either.

Spinning, she ran back to the shed and halted at the door. Whitson's body still lay slumped on the floor. Drina paused, trembling and shaking. She had to pass close by him to reach her backpack.

A shot rang out, galvanizing her into action. Leaping over Whitson, she stuffed the money into her backpack, slid the computer in on top, flung the straps over her shoulders and hurried back to the door.

As she crossed to Norwood's small car, she heard another shot. She slid into the seat but could barely reach the pedals.

No time to move the seat closer. She grasped the wheel, shoved the gearshift into Reverse and shot backward.

Slipping all the way back against the seat, she almost ran the car into a ditch. The briefcase on the passenger seat flew through the air and landed on her lap. She shoved it aside and pulled herself forward, then slammed on the brakes, pushed the gearshift into Drive and spun the steering wheel in the direction of the equipment.

This time she was prepared when the car hit the slight ditch on the side of the road. The unlatched door flapped open…closed… open again. She gripped the wheel tighter and gunned the engine. The car jumped into the air. When it came down, her foot jammed onto the gas pedal and the engine revved.

Carter, who still faced the culvert, heard the noise and spun.

Drina cried out as he aimed the gun in her direction and fired. She ducked to the side, leaning out the open door. The bullet shattered the windshield. The car slowed almost to a stop. Drina saw Carter through the crack in the swaying door. He marched forward, taking aim again. Soon he'd be close enough to hit her. Drina pushed the gas again. The car was only a few feet from the edge. It would be over the side in seconds.

Reaching across, she tugged the briefcase down onto the floorboard, directly onto the gas pedal, and rolled out the door. She hit the dirt hard, but turned quickly to see the car shooting straight toward Carter. He lunged away and fell backward over the side of the hill. The sound of twisting metal and shattering glass echoed through the culvert before the motor stopped abruptly.

Drina sagged against the ground. Taking a deep breath, she sucked up dust and felt grit on her lips. Trying to catch her breath, she rolled onto her backpack and looked up to see the blue sky fading into twilight.

She needed to get up. Carter might come marching over the hill any moment, pointing his wicked gun right at her. But she couldn't move. Couldn't force her body into action, even when she heard another motor close by.

She opened her eyes as the quad spun around next to her, kicking dust in the air. Norwood extended his hand.

"Come on. Let's get out of here."

The half smile floating over those oh-so-perfect lips gave her the reassuring charge of energy she needed. She gripped his hand. He pulled her up and she climbed onto the back.

"Hang on tight. It's going to get bumpy."

Drina wrapped her arms around his waist. With her cheek pressed against his warm, strong back, only one thought went through her mind.

We're safe. We're safe. We're safe.

Norwood gave the quad gas. Dirt and

gravel spun out behind the big wheels as he headed toward the road. Drina had to loosen her hold slightly as they hit bumps, but not too much.

She wasn't sure why he'd betrayed his partners in crime…especially since he'd probably leaked the information that led to her kidnapping in the first place. Was he hoping to sell her plan and pocket the money for himself? Or was he on her side? Was that why he had risked his life to save her? She wasn't certain but right now his strong, sturdy body was the only solid, stable thing in an exploding world. She clung to him with all her might.

The ATV reached the dirt road leading back to town. They dipped down into the culvert and started to climb the other side. Drina glanced back at the shed and the pile of equipment behind it. Still no sign of Carter. They were safe, really safe.

With that thought, they crested the hill and a helicopter surged in the air directly in front of them.

The black machine hovered above, menacing, kicking up wind and gravel. Drina squinted and narrowed her gaze just as a man in dark clothing leaned out of the side, a long rifle poised in his hands.

"Hang on!" Norwood yelled and turned

so fast, Drina almost slid off the side of the quad. A series of wind turbines were located along the ridge to their right. The turbines rose over two hundred feet in the air, and the blades were over a hundred feet wide. The helicopter couldn't follow them into the clustered turbines of the wind farm. If Norwood could put enough distance between them and the helicopter, they might be out of the rifle's range.

Drina clung to his back, trying to remember the range of a rifle. She worked with weapons. She was sure ranges were one of the useless details she'd picked up over the years, but for the life of her, she couldn't put her finger on a number.

Figures were safe. She knew numbers like she knew her own name but even they deserted her as she hung on to a man she thought was a traitor and hurtled over a narrow ridge, expecting to feel a bullet pierce her back at any moment.

They reached the first turbine and Norwood jerked the ATV sharply to the left. A bullet pinged the side of the turbine's tower and bounced away. Zigzagging erratically, Norwood made it to the next tower before another bullet hit, this time striking the ground where they'd been moments ago. Drina flinched and glanced back.

The helicopter wavered up and down in the darkening sky, then adjusted so the sniper could take aim.

Where was the ever-present desert wind? Why did the gusts fade now when they needed them most? Drina heard the crack of another shot and cringed. She ducked, hunching up against Norwood, her body pressed against his. The *zing* whistled by, too close for comfort, and struck the metal turbine ahead of them... A direct hit.

Norwood jerked to the side, sinking down into the narrow gully below them. There were tall turbines on the ridge across and behind them. The helicopter couldn't follow or come up on the other side. Another bullet struck the side of the hill but it was off. The marksmen in the helicopter couldn't site them this deep in the gully.

The gulch's bottom was too narrow for the quad's wheelbase so Norwood was forced to zigzag up and down the sides. Their wavering path slowed their escape. Still, the sound of the helicopter came from farther and farther above them. Drina couldn't look up. All of her concentration was focused on hanging on to Norwood's slender waist as their path dipped and rose along the bumpy gully bottom.

Eventually it opened into a wider culvert and they entered the sandy bottom of a small stream. Their path straightened. The sound of the helicopter faded away as darkness settled over them. Norwood traveled a long time before switching on the quad's headlights.

The beams shot across the streambed, lighting bushes and rocks as they traveled deeper and deeper into the desert. Drina had no idea where they were headed. She only knew they were traveling far away from town and any kind of help. After a while, her grip loosened.

A mile. That was the average range of a rifle. Funny how the number jumped into her mind now.

I must be beginning to relax. This time we're safe. Really safe... At least for the time being.

At the moment she didn't care. Only two things mattered. Her back wasn't shivering in reflexive fear of being shot, and the man in front of her was strong, confident and sure. He might still be a traitor to their country, but he'd risked his life to save her, covering her body with his and returning for her when he could have made his own escape. Right now nothing else mattered. She pressed her face into Norwood's back and closed her eyes.

Odd thoughts came to her. The faint scent of lemony aftershave. She'd watched Norwood dive into dirt, run up and down a rocky ravine and scramble for his life, but still he managed to smell good. It seemed a silly thing to think about, especially since he'd betrayed everything Drina tried to accomplish. But somehow, the man made her feel safe. Protected.

Right now Cal Norwood was the man of steel, larger than life, invincible...but he smelled like lemon sunshine.

Another silly detail that lodged in her mind: she could wrap her arms around his entire waist and hold tight. How could such a slender torso manhandle this jostling, shimmying vehicle?

The question faded in her mind as they hit a bump. Drina grasped him tighter and snuggled close, burying her face in his leather jacket.

Shock. It must be shock bringing all these crazy, mixed-up thoughts to her mind. Joy at being alive must have heightened her senses because Drina was definitely not the type to romanticize. But right now it didn't matter.

They were safe and Norwood was wonderful. That was all that mattered for the moment.

Drina lost track of time. They drove for what seemed like hours. The stream widened again into a dry riverbed. Above them on the bank, the headlights flashed on a black strip that looked like a paved road. After a while, Norwood slowed the quad to a stop and turned the light toward the bank. The brown crest of a small hut appeared above them. Norwood eased the quad into the V of some boulders along the riverbed and shut down the engine.

Drina's ears and body vibrated for a moment more, adjusting to the sudden stillness. The wind had picked up and carried a biting edge. She shivered. Norwood held out his hand again.

"We need to find shelter so we can rest for a bit."

Rest? We need to find help.

Drina wanted to speak but her teeth started to chatter and her body trembled. Overwhelmed by the sudden shaking, she took his warm, secure hand, and he pulled her up the bank. Her legs were sore from being bound and weak from the long ride on the quad. She could hardly force them to move. By the time they reached the top, she was out of breath.

The small building was a brown tollbooth in the center of a divided road.

"Wh-what is this place?" She barely got the words out between shudders.

"It's Red Rock Canyon, a state park for ATV riders. It's been closed for several years. Cutbacks."

He hurried across the asphalt road and pushed on the locked door. Gripping her arms tight against her, Drina watched him jam his shoulder into the flimsy door several times.

"Wh-why don't you just break the w-window and unlock it?"

"It wouldn't give us much shelter from the wind then, would it? Besides, I don't want to leave too much damage behind. It will make for an easy trail to follow."

With that, he gave the door a sturdy kick and it bounced open. He pulled Drina inside and tucked her into a corner.

"Have a seat and I'll see if I can't find a water faucet outside."

Nodding, Drina bumped up against the wall and slid to the floor. Inside, out of the cold wind, felt so much better. Slipping her backpack off, she sighed with relief, but the sigh turned into a sob…and the trembling continued. She couldn't control the shaking and suddenly, a thought jumped into her mind.

When she'd first met Norwood, she'd mentally made fun of his strict adherence to rules and the impression he gave off that he could save the world. Well…he'd just saved Drina and everything in her world. Hot tears of shame and relief rolled down her cheeks.

Norwood returned to the shed and slipped inside, out of the cold wind. He placed a large rock against the door to hold it shut. "There are faucets outside but all the water is turned off."

His only answer was a sob-like sound. He turned. Tears sparkled on Drina's cheeks.

"I—I can't stop." She seemed barely able to get the words out.

Cal dropped to the ground beside her. It was her fault she was here. Her own disregard for security had resulted in her kidnapping. Still, her statement sounded so pathetic, he couldn't stop himself. Reaching across the space, he put an arm around her. His gesture seemed to release a flood of emotion. She spilled into his arms so suddenly, Cal was caught off guard and his arms spread wide as she wrapped hers around his waist.

He could almost feel Drina's pent-up emotions washing out of her. It felt awkward, uncomfortable…as if he sat chest deep in a sea of feelings he didn't need or understand.

Then she reached up, wrapped chilly fingers around his neck and buried her cold cheeks and nose in the curve of his neck. Skin to skin. Life to life.

This he understood. This need he knew well. Basic needs. Men and women. Even her sobs reminded them both that they were alive. He enfolded her in his arms and held her close while hot tears soaked his shirt.

He'd studied this woman, knew her schedule, her goals. He knew more about her than about any other woman. But he'd never been this close, never held her in his arms. Somehow she felt right. He'd also seen the terror in her eyes as she lay on the floor of the shack. That image flashed through his mind, and a wave of tenderness he couldn't explain washed over him. He pressed his lips to the top of her head.

Her breakdown only lasted a minute or two. Then he felt boundaries going up, brick by brick, as she sealed her emotions inside once again. After another moment or so, her hand pulled away. She wiped the dampness from her cheeks.

Truth be told, Cal was disappointed. Her waiflike figure contained some pretty soft curves. It felt good to hold something real, something soft and gentle. Not just basic instincts but something more. For too long, his life had been all about emptiness and sharp edges. Drina was a sudden reminder that there was more to life. Thankfully, they were both still alive to enjoy it. Cal allowed himself a moment to appreciate the gift.

But only a moment. The fact remained that they were in this mess thanks to Drina's willful disregard for security protocols. His mission was destroyed and both their lives were in danger.

In spite of the fact that she was still trembling, he pushed her away.

She wiped at wet cheeks again and sniffled. "I've soaked your shirt." Her voice sounded hoarse and rough.

"It'll dry." His tone was brusque. He needed to shake the unexpected effects of her nearness. He didn't want to but he had to give her credit. "You were incredibly quick thinking back there. I owe you. You saved my life when you drove that car at Carter."

Her motions suddenly stilled. "Did I k-kill him?"

"No. But he did have to jump away quickly and you gave me the pleasure of watching him tumble head over heels down the hill.

I've wanted to do something like that for two years."

She straightened and gazed into his face. Moonlight poured in from the large windows above them, lighting her pert nose and lips, puffy from crying…red lips that seemed very kissable.

"Norwood, are you a traitor?"

All thoughts of kissing disappeared and his ire rose. The snarky scientist was popping up again. Ms. Gallagher was nothing if not unpredictable. "You should call me by my first name if you're going to accuse me of something so terrible."

She didn't miss a beat. "Cal, are you a traitor?"

His jaw tightened "Always quick thinking. I see why they call you the wonder kid."

"That's not an answer."

Leaning back against the wall, he shook his head. "No. I'm not a traitor. In fact, the consensus with my team was that you were the traitor."

"Me? Why in the world would they suspect me?"

"You made it easy with your disregard for protocol and careless attitude toward security. Information was leaking out and the biggest holes in the safety net were around you."

She hung her head. "I never took it seriously until…"

"Until it almost got you killed."

She looked away. "I never meant for that to happen."

Regret was deep in her tone. It struck a chord with Cal. "You know, I believe you mean that. But it doesn't change the fact that we're here because of your carelessness."

"My work… My project means everything to me."

Irritation filtered through him. "It better. You almost lost your life over it."

Her gaze darted to the backpack lying beside them, but she said nothing more. For the first time he realized she'd had the nerve to retrieve her computer…and the money. His respect for her rose a little, but it didn't change their situation.

"Maybe someday you'll tell me why your work means so much you'd willingly risk your life and the lives of others. But right now we need to concentrate on getting out of here alive."

He pulled his cell phone out of his pocket and plugged in the password. Bright light filled the small booth. He heard a small sigh of what sounded like relief…until he started to power the phone down.

"What are you doing? Why don't you call for help?"

"Because I'm not sure who to call. We knew—"

"Hold on. Who is we? Your security team at the base?"

"No. I'm an undercover agent for the CIA."

"CIA?" Her expression phased through several emotions in an instant—shock, confusion and then disgust. Cal couldn't tell if the last was directed at him or his company.

She frowned. "That can't be. You're head of base security."

"Security chief is my cover. I'm the field operator for a team in Washington. We've been following the activities of an arms dealer by the name of Alexi Gorkoff, trying to find his source. He's been buying top secret weapons on the black market for several years. We finally narrowed his contacts down to someone on the inside. A person at your home lab or here on the support team of the base has been selling plans even before they're completed."

"Bill, my boss, mentioned something to me about a security problem a while back. But I thought it was in the aeronautics department, not mine."

"It's all departments and all projects, which indicates someone high up in the chain of command. The CIA planted me in the base's security force to find the leak. We created a background for me, which included a substantial gambling debt. I let it be known that I was willing to do anything to pay it off. A man approached me and we started feeding him information. After two years of work, I was finally going to meet the boss."

"Whitson and Carter were talking about their leader. They said he gave the order to kidnap me."

"Whoever he is, he's clever about covering his tracks. He throws suspicion onto unsuspecting people like you. We… I wasted months tracking down the wrong people. Every time I'd get close to the truth, he'd disappear again."

"So when you walked in and saw me lying there, you had to make a choice between meeting the boss and saving my life." Her voice was low and raspy.

His jaw tightened unit it was almost painful. "You didn't leave me much choice, Drina. I thought they might have already finished you off and dropped your body down an abandoned mine shaft somewhere out here in the desert. It's happened before."

An image of the young man who disappeared flashed into his mind. He was a computer geek with glasses…much like Drina's. He had serious social issues and hadn't been very popular with his coworkers. The CIA had already pegged him as a potential spy before Cal came on the scene. But in Cal's quest to convince the members of the black market ring that he was willing to do anything for money, he'd fed them erroneous information. The leaked info countered real intel from the young computer geek. He'd disappeared two days later, never to be found, his body probably dumped down one of the many abandoned mine shafts in the endless desert floor.

Cal had taken the kid's disappearance personally. He would have felt the same about Drina if he'd found her dead. Still…

He shook his head in a sharp movement. "If you'd just followed the protocols, we wouldn't be here now."

His words seemed to make Drina aware of her disheveled state. She sifted fingers through her short hair—hair that, in spite of all she'd been through, was still shiny black, tousled but touchable. A twig or leaf had wedged itself into a lock near the top. He remembered its silky feel against his lips and itched to pull the leaf loose just to feel that shiny curl.

"You don't know anything about me. You don't know how important my work is."

Her words squelched his soft feelings. "I know your work was important enough to try to protect it. Besides, I've made it my business to know about you. MIT graduate after only three years. Top honors. Recruited by Aero Electronics right out of school."

Her lips parted in surprise. After a moment she looked away. "And that's where the interesting part ends. Now my life is all work."

"True, but you were a social butterfly in college. Served on the board of every club you joined. You even volunteered with Boston's poorest, in soup kitchens and eventually in hospice, serving the aged and dying. That really intrigued me. To be honest, it filled me with admiration."

He leaned his head back against the wall. "A young woman like you, taking on the most difficult situations life has to offer. But something happened. You changed. Dropped your volunteer work to focus on your studies, graduated earlier and went on to a career in electronic warfare. What happened, Drina?"

Maybe shock had loosened Drina's previously tight-lipped attitude. To Cal's surprise she answered him.

"I fell in love."

THREE

Moonlight fell onto her face, softening her features. Wide-eyed. Wounded. She looked so very lovely and so vulnerable.

That's how love looks on Drina Gallagher. Cal couldn't take his gaze away. The shock of that look, that softness, jolted him. Drina was so very beautiful with the silver light kissing her eyelashes and dark hair. The urge to comfort her, to pull her into his arms almost overwhelmed him.

Get a grip, Cal. She's here because of her own disregard for security. Still, the need to comfort her was almost irresistible.

She saved him from making a fool of himself when she raised both knees and wrapped her arms around them, gripping tight. "His name was John. He was…good. A rule follower… A lot like you, actually." She glanced at him but he couldn't define the look in her gaze. Was it admiration or scorn?

"What happened?"

"We broke up. My parents didn't approve. They were right, of course. We were too young…too idealistic and foolish."

"I don't think following the rules or being idealistic makes you foolish."

"Does quitting school and joining the marines qualify?" The sarcasm in her tone lashed at Cal, made him scale back his reaction. Her attitude said much about the depth of her feelings for an event that had occurred years ago. Obviously, there was more she wasn't saying.

"Perhaps," he said cautiously, "or maybe it speaks about his patriotism and desire to serve."

"John died in Afghanistan. He was twenty-two years old. His death was a complete waste…just a waste."

Cal was silent for a long while. "I understand your feelings but I can't draw the connection. Your first love died in battle, so now you build weapons?"

Wrong thing to say. Drina bristled like a dog on alert and went on the attack. "What about you? Why do you work for the CIA?"

"There are lots of ways to serve, Drina."

"I'm building weapons to save lives. All the CIA does is plot and kill people."

His jaw tightened. "Sometimes we save lives, too. Like this afternoon."

His reminder took the spit and vinegar out of her. She lay her forehead on top of her knees. Her next words were muffled. "You're right. I'm sorry. I just—I'm not cut out for this." Her words came out less belligerent. "Even if I wanted to do it, I couldn't. I'm falling to pieces."

"I had a breakdown after my first encounter with evil." His tone came out bitter. "It's natural."

"Evil?" She raised her head. "You're a Christian, aren't you?"

He nodded.

"I should have known. John was, too." She slumped again, this time turning sideways with her cheek on her knees. She sagged with a weariness that went deeper than the physical. Cal recognized spiritual conflict when he saw it. He was on intimate terms with those battles, battles that helped him to anticipate her next question.

"But you're still working for the agency. Why?"

"A lot of prayer. No matter how many times I asked God to send me in another direction, He didn't. After a while, I had to accept that I was where He wanted me to be. Then my pastor advised me to count the lives I saved, not the lost ones."

Good advice, but it hadn't helped much when he remembered the men who killed Buddy were still free...and still killing.

Drina studied him in the dim shadows of the tollbooth. He could feel her gaze—intense, probing.

"Do you think Whitson is dead?"

He gave a tight sigh. "I'm a pretty good shot. I don't think he'll be kidnapping anyone else."

In the silver moonlight her lips thinned. "I don't think I could do it...justify killing."

Anger flared. "You're right. I should have let Whitson shoot you."

She sagged. "I'm sorry. I'm very thankful you didn't. I'm just trying to understand."

"That's your problem. You think too much. There was nothing to understand. It was you or him. I chose you."

She met his gaze, her eyes wide. "You're right again. Thank you."

"You're welcome." He brushed dirt off his jeans, his movements angry and abrupt. He tried to hold back his irritation but it didn't work. "You don't make sense. All this complaining about death but you work for a defense company, specifically in weapons."

"Weapons that protect men, stop the fighting by shutting their electronics down."

"It also causes the soldier's skin to feel like it's on fire."

"Yes, it does sensitize their nerves, but it causes no permanent damage. As soon as it shuts off, the pain goes away. It's a nonlethal weapon. No one dies."

Cal was silent for a few minutes before he nodded. "So that's what drives you. Saving lives."

"Yes. Saving lives. Making up for those John would have saved if he'd lived."

She looked away, but even in the dark shadows he could see the determined set of her jaw. He was more than surprised. Their goals were the same, yet she objected to everything he did and fought him every step of the way. Even when he was saving her life.

Drina Gallagher was a puzzle...one he didn't have the time to solve. He needed to get her to a safe place so he could get back to the business of finding the boss and his gang.

He ran a hand around his neck. "It's a good plan, Drina. Your work is valuable. So let's see what we can do about getting you and your plans back into the right hands. The question is, who can we trust?"

"My boss. Bill Carlisle. I trust him implicitly."

"Do you? Who did you call when you discovered the key to this new weapon?"

"Well, Bill, of course."

"So he was the only one who knew you'd found the solution."

"Yes, but someone else was on the line. I heard the double clicks and Bill even cautioned me not to reveal my location. Not that it did any good. They already knew where I was. The point is, I know I can trust Bill."

"Let's pray you're right."

"You pray. I'll rely on my own judgment." She averted her gaze.

He studied her for a long time. Drina definitely had God issues. He suspected her unwillingness to relinquish control was a symptom of some deep-seated anger with God—maybe even the source of her resentment toward Cal's work. But she refused to say more…even to make eye contact.

He shook his head. "Right now I need to make sure they can't track us through my phone. I hope it's not already too late."

They'd talked so long his phone had timed out. He punched the pass code in again. Light flared and Cal powered all the way down. Drina raised her head to watch him. Moonlight fell over her features and he watched hope drain out of her as the phone's light faded.

"Why can't we just call the local sheriff's department?"

"Because the authorities will have to contact my superiors or your company, and the boss's men will be able to trace us. It'll be a race to see who reaches us first. Judging from previous experience, I'm counting on the bad guys."

"Won't the CIA wonder why you aren't contacting them?"

"I was going deep undercover, remember? They didn't expect to hear from me for days. They won't risk betraying my cover."

"No, *I* did that for you."

She was right—her carelessness and single-minded obsession were the reasons they were here. Still, her tone revealed deep regret. For all of her strong opinions and scathing tongue, Drina Gallagher cared…more than she was willing to admit. He was glad. Her tone and the fact that they had the same goal softened his attitude.

"We saved each other. We actually made a pretty good team."

She laughed. It was a small sound, like she didn't do it much. But it was light and sweet. He liked it.

"You and I… A team? Do you know how illogical that sounds? We're exact opposites."

He shrugged. "Illogical or not, here we are. And we did good. We're alive."

She nodded slowly, her head still balanced on her knees. "Yes. We're alive." She lifted her head. "So what are *we* going to do?"

"We have to get back to the base. I need to see what's happening, who is moving and how." He paused, then almost as an after-thought, added, "Then we'll ask for help."

"How are we going to do that? Drive right up to the gates on our quad?" Her tone told Cal she meant her explanation to be facetious. But it wasn't.

"Not through the gates but across the desert, so no one will see us. We can ditch the quad and sneak into my place. I'll be able to connect to my phone and emails, maybe even my office computer."

Her lips parted in surprise. "You mean it? We could just drive across the desert to the base?"

"If Carter and the others on his team don't find us—and I don't think they will—they'll expect us to alert the authorities, not to stay quiet and double back to the base. So that's exactly what we'll do, the unexpected. We could be safely ensconced at my place with no one the wiser."

Drina closed her eyes. "I wish we were there now."

"I can't risk trying to find my way in the dark. We'll have to wait until daylight. The park is closed for camping, but just outside its boundaries is a wide-open valley that belongs to the Bureau of Land Management. I'm sure we'll find campers and ATV riders there. We'll mix in with them, cross the park and head out the opposite direction...to California City. We can gas up there." He pointed to her backpack. "Fortunately, someone had enough sense to bring along some cash. Maybe we can get something to eat before we cross the desert to the base."

Drina shivered. "You make it sound so easy."

"It will be if everything goes well."

She closed her eyes. "The best thing you said was something to eat. I'm starving right now."

"You should be. It's been over twenty-four hours since you ate and you need some water." He glanced at her backpack again, "You wouldn't happen—"

"I do." She brightened and dragged the bag toward her. "I usually keep a granola bar…" She unzipped the side bag and triumphantly held up the mixed-nut-and-raisin treat. "We can share it." She ripped open the wrapping and broke it in half, but Cal shook his head.

"I had breakfast and lunch today. You need it more than I do."

"Are you sure?"

He nodded. "You'll need your strength to hang on if we're going to cross the desert. But I might share some water. Do you have a bottle stashed in there someplace?"

With her mouth full, she nodded and unzipped the other side. She handed him the bottle as she chewed.

Seeing her slow, troubled chewing, Cal took a swig and handed it over. "Finish it off. Like I said, you'll need it."

She took the bottle and did as he suggested. The food and drink took some of the edge off her attitude. When she finished she leaned her forehead on her knees again.

"You should try to rest. You'll need it for tomorrow."

"I can't. I'm too cold."

Not waiting for her to tell him no, Cal took off his leather jacket and wrapped it around her. Drina nestled her nose into a fold and sighed with relief.

"Wake up, Drina."

Cal's voice came to her through an exhausted mist.

He shook her roughly.

"Wake up! Get moving now!"

"What—what is it?"

"I think they found us. They must have had a trace on my cell phone."

The booth was pitch-dark. Even the moon had abandoned them. Wind buzzed through the building like an angry bee. The sound reminded Drina of the metal shack beneath the wind turbines, and adrenaline surged through her.

She grabbed her backpack. As she slid it over her shoulders, she heard the far-off whine of engines…running at high speed in the dark.

No one on a fun weekend would be racing their engines and risking an accident in the dark.

A freezing blast hit Drina in the face when Cal pulled the rock away from the door. If not for the tug of his hand, she might have tumbled back into the booth.

The moon had disappeared behind a cover

of black, billowy storm clouds. Drina raced across the asphalt road with Cal. Icy wind pierced through her jacket as they slip-slid down the bank and onto the quad.

Her heart skipped a beat as Cal hit the ignition. The motor ground without turning over. He turned the handle twice, pumping the gas, and still the engine wouldn't ignite.

"Hop off!" Cal yelled over the whistling gusts. He pushed the quad out from the protection of the boulders and rocked it back and forth.

"It's got plenty of gas. That's not the problem." He scooted back on and pumped the gas handle again.

Drina shifted from foot to foot and looked down the dimly lit streambed. She couldn't see anything, but that meant nothing. The men on those quads could be right around the corner, hidden in the dark.

"Please. Please. Let it start."

The whispered words were torn from her lips and lost in the wind…but the engine turned over and revved. Wincing with relief, she climbed on the back and Cal gunned the gas, spraying sand behind them as he took off upstream.

He said something but she couldn't make it out over the wailing wind. Something about headlights. He must have said he didn't want to risk turning them on. She looked behind again but saw only inky blackness. The men following them must be traveling without lights, too, but she heard the ever-increasing hum of their engines.

Cal guided the quad steadily down the riverbed, swerving to avoid rocks and tree limbs, some half-buried in the sand. He hit a deep cleft and almost bounced Drina off the back. Suppressing a grimace of pain as her bottom bounced on the metal bar at the back, she pulled herself forward and held on tighter.

She couldn't look back now without turning and loosening her hold, but she could see ahead. High in the mountains above, lightning flashed across the ebony sky, followed by the boom of thunder.

The wind faded momentarily and Drina heard Cal counting between the streaks of lightning and cannon-like thunder.

"That storm is closer than it looks."

Drina nodded. The air vibrated with the overwhelming power of the thunder. Even the boulders seemed to shiver with each clap. And in the momentary silence after each boom, they heard the engines close behind them.

The higher they climbed, the larger the

rocks in the streambed became. Cal was having a hard time guiding the quad between them. Drina slid from one side to the other and bounced until her teeth rattled. She clung to Cal, wishing they could find a path out of the ravine, but the sides were steep and lined with boulders.

Then Cal hit a deep rivulet and the quad came to a dead stop, nearly toppling both of them over the handlebars.

Cal was off in a flash. "Help me rock it out."

Drina climbed behind and tried to push the big quad. She couldn't even budge it.

"We have to work together. On my count. One…two…three…pull."

Her feet slid out behind her. Her backpack was tugging her off balance. She slid it off her shoulders and hooked it on the seat.

"Ready?"

She nodded. Cal counted. This time the quad rocked. "Again, Drina. We're getting it."

"One…two…"

Another sound rose over the wind, halting Cal midcount. They looked around.

"What is that?"

Cal didn't answer. He stood still, poised.

The noise came from upriver. It sounded closer and whooshed…like water.

"It's a flash flood. We have to get out of this streambed. Now!" Cal ran toward the boulder-strewn incline. Drina froze, her gaze fixed on the quad, their only means of escape.

"Leave it, Drina. Run!"

She didn't move.

Cal lunged back and grabbed her hand just as a ten-foot wave of muddy brown water surged around the corner. As Cal dragged her toward the bank, Drina looked behind. She'd left her backpack on the seat of the quad.

She couldn't risk letting it wash downriver straight into the hands of the men following them. Jerking free, she ran back for it.

Drina's feet skidded in the sand. The wave was thirty feet away, traveling with the force of a train. She jerked the backpack loose and bolted for the side of the river.

Already halfway up the riverbank, Cal motioned her to hurry. She could see his lips moving, but she couldn't hear over the roaring water.

He stretched out his hand. With one last leap, she jumped toward the bank. A warm, strong grasp pulled her up just as the edge of the wave swept her feet out from beneath her. She screamed as her body pulled downstream along with the rush of mud and water. If not for Cal's grip on her hand…

A frantic peek over her shoulder revealed their quad, tumbling end over end down the riverbed.

Cal braced his feet and gave another hearty tug.

"Give me your other hand."

She couldn't think, couldn't speak, as the freezing water tore at her shoes, trying to pull her down into the swirling miasma. But she shook her head. No way was she letting go of her computer.

Cal made a frustrated sound and jerked her upward. Drina's arm felt like it might come out of its socket, but she wouldn't let go of the laptop.

She felt a rock beneath her foot and pushed, surging upward. Cal cupped beneath her armpits and pulled her all the way up and over his body, completely out of the water. She lay on top of him, both of them gasping.

At last, Cal released her, but Drina wasn't ready to let go. She gripped his jacket with her now-free hand and buried her face against his chest. He was so warm. So strong. So safe.

So angry. She could feel it in the taut tension of his body. He didn't speak for a long while. When he did, fury colored his tone an angry red.

"That was stupid, Drina. Those plans are not more valuable than your life."

She looked up. His eyes flashed blue silver like lightning. His jaw was tight, and a pulse throbbed on one side of his neck. He was furious and all she wanted to do was bury her face in the curve of his neck and feel life beating through him.

But her plans *were* more important than her life. Her plans for that weapon would save so many lives, lives much more valuable than hers. But she didn't say the words out loud. Didn't speak…couldn't speak at all. After a few moments he gripped her arms and rolled her to the side.

Cold emptiness washed over her. All she wanted was to crawl back into the warm safety of his arms. But the look on his face stopped her.

Jerking the backpack out of her hands, he opened it, pulled out her powered-down cell phone, the money and the computer, then tossed the backpack into the river.

She reached for it. "Hey! What are you doing?"

Cal held her back with an extended arm. "I should have left it on the floor of the hut. They probably planted a tracker somewhere inside while you were unconscious. Carter wouldn't have taken a chance on losing the computer or the money. He would have given himself a safety net, a way to track it."

Taut, frustrated tension filled his tone. But Drina couldn't tell if it was directed toward himself or her. Either way, she had no intention of pushing him more. She sealed her lips shut even though her wallet, computer power cord and favorite lip balm were floating away on the river of muddy water.

An angry Cal was impressive…kind of like the storm. His low tone made her more aware than shouting. His silent anger should have frightened her but in some crazy way it had the opposite effect. She was drawn to it. He vibrated with power like a force of nature. She wanted to grasp the arm pressed against her waist, to feel that taut, tense strength, but she also feared the explosion that type of gesture might bring.

Just hours ago that same power had been unleashed and a man had died because of Cal's actions. Even though his efforts had saved her life, Drina couldn't quite reconcile herself to the death. Who she was and everything she did was about saving lives. Taking one—or watching one being taken—rattled her beyond words…and so did the man who had done the killing.

Subdued by her own tumultuous thoughts and reactions, she leaned back on the rock and tried to slow her breathing. Cal did the same but all too soon, he rose.

Cal stuffed the banded money into his pockets. "We need to get going. If we made it out of the riverbed, those men probably did, too."

Without looking at her, he strode up and over the edge of the rocky bank. He didn't look back but he heard her climb to her feet and follow. Each time she took a step her soaked-through shoes and socks squished. Sandy grit had to be grinding beneath her heel and the sides of her shoes.

He waited at the top but still didn't look at her. One glance at her face, and he might unleash all of his pent-up frustration. He'd destroyed his mission and risked his own life to save hers, and in almost the next moment, she chose to jump in front of a raging flash flood. The woman was beyond his comprehension. He could barely contain his rage. So he kept his gaze focused on the hill in front of them. Only when Drina came up beside him, shoes squishing with each step, did he look down.

"You're going to have blisters in minutes." He strode to a nearby rock and sat down.

"Take off your socks and wear mine. Your shoes will soak through but at least it will buy us some time. Hopefully we can reach the campground and I'll decide what to do then."

Drina dropped to a nearby rock. "What do you mean, *decide what to do*? Can't we just ask one of the campers to help us?"

He chanced a glance at her then. Her teeth chattered and she shivered. Cal clamped his jaw tighter, determined not to let her discomfort ease his anger.

"You don't know Carter and those men. No one has ever been able to identify them because they don't leave behind any witnesses... ever. If we ask for help, we're risking that person's life, too. It's better just to work on our own."

"B-but what can we do without the quad?"

She stripped off her shoes and socks, then rolled up her jeans. The pants twisted into a narrow, wet band just below her knees.

Cal tossed her his socks. She caught them midair and quickly slid them over her dainty feet. Angry with himself for noticing, he gritted his teeth and looked away.

"I'll figure something out." It would be hard to do considering the fact that he wanted to strangle her. Anger and attraction warred inside him although he didn't understand how he could be attracted to her. She didn't even *like* him. But he would put both emotions aside and figure out their next move. He had to.

Sliding bare feet into his shoes, he stalked away. Moments later Drina followed him.

They crested the hill and Cal paused. A valley maybe ten miles wide lay beneath them. Below, they could just make out the white shapes of various types of campers gathered in four or five groupings across the expanse. Cal spotted large motor homes, trucks and trailers with ramps at the back.

"I've never seen those." Drina pointed to the closest grouping with several of the trailers. "What are they?"

"They're called toy haulers. They're designed to provide accommodations for eating and sleeping in the front and an empty back end to load with ATVs."

Cal headed down the hill, straight for the closest caravan of toy haulers. He didn't look back but he sensed Drina close behind. The grouped vehicles couldn't have been more than three or four miles away. Still, by the time they reached the security of some nearby rock covering, daylight had turned the eastern sky gray.

Cal motioned for Drina to sit. She didn't

hesitate—just placed her back against the boulder, slid all the way down, folded her knees up and rested her head against the roll of wet jeans on her knees. He caught a glimpse of her wrists. They were cut and ir-ritated from the zip ties. He suspected she was losing it fast. If she didn't get some more substantial food and rest soon…

He had to resist the urge to pull her close and shore up her sagging strength. What was it about this woman that triggered all of his protective instincts? She didn't want his help—and didn't deserve it, after ignoring all of the safeguards he and everyone else had tried to put in place—but he couldn't seem to resist the urge to shelter her. If he wasn't care-ful those urges would get them both killed.

Besides, he had a job to do. He had to stop the boss and his men. Buddy and too many other people had already lost their lives to this gang. Cal had penetrated further into the group than anyone else. He was close…within reach of discovering the boss's identity. He absolutely could not let these mixed-up feel-ings distract him. Gritting his teeth, he fo-cused on the closest toy hauler.

Drina lifted her head from her knees. "Did you come up with a plan yet?"

"Shhh…"

Eyes wide, Drina scrambled to her feet to look over the rock. A door opened with a squeak. A man with jeans and a sweatshirt exited. In the gray light, he walked to the back of the trailer, released the locks and lowered the back-end ramp, revealing a large quad. Along the front wall of the space was a sink, a small table and a bed.

Another man came out of a nearby trailer and joined the first. Cal and Drina were close enough to hear the men's quiet, sunrise conversation.

"Still going home early, Jake?"

"Yeah. No point in fighting a bad carburetor and the rain. I can't ride and I don't expect we'll be spending much time around the campfire with this weather."

The other man chuckled. "True. But you're going to miss some epic mud rides."

Jake shook his head. "I worked on that carburetor till almost two last night without success. But if I leave early enough, I might be able to get my quad in to Sharkey's Repair before noon. Hopefully he'll have it back to me in time to ride next weekend."

"Good idea. Want me to help you load up?"

"Thanks."

The two men gathered some lawn chairs

and red plastic gas cans. Within a few minutes Jake pushed up the ramp and locked it.

"The wife's got a pot of coffee on the stove.
Can I offer you a cup for the road?"

"Sounds great. Let me get my travel mug."
Jake entered the door of the trailer on the
side facing Cal and Drina. After a few minutes he came back out, locked the door and
checked it.

Cal pointed to a large creosote bush about
twenty feet away. "Do you see that covering?"

Drina nodded.

"When I signal, stay low, move as quietly
as possible and make a run for it."

He waited until Jake rounded the corner of
his trailer and disappeared from view.

"Go." Cal's harsh whisper sent adrenaline
pumping through his limbs. His legs felt like
lead and he almost tripped twice as he ducked
and ran, swerving around clumps of tumble-
weeds and rocks. When he reached the shelter of the trailer, he glanced back. Where was
Drina?

Panic made a hot dash through his blood-
stream, and his gaze shot around the clearing. She was hunched behind a nearby bush.
Mentally kicking himself for wasting time

looking for her, he pulled his tools out of his pocket and began to work the lock.

The handle turned and the door opened. Drina gasped. One finger against his lips, Cal motioned her forward. She ducked again and ran toward the trailer. Fortunately, the large toy hauler blocked them from the view of the other campers.

Cal grasped her elbow. "Move carefully. Don't rock the trailer with heavy steps."

She nodded, then gingerly made her way in. Cal eased the door closed and motioned to the table booth directly across from them. He pointed to the floor.

"Brace yourself. It'll be a bumpy ride. Don't make any sudden movements or sounds."

Drina nodded again.

In a few moments Jake and his friend approached the trailer, their voices easily understood in the quiet morning.

Drina caught her breath when they stopped right outside the door. Cal grasped her arm and gave a shake of his head.

"Drive safe, buddy. See you Monday."

"Yeah. Enjoy some of that mud for me."

The other man laughed and then the truck door opened and the engine roared to life. Drina breathed a sigh of relief, then sucked it back in when the trailer jerked forward.

She bounced a foot into the air and landed with a thump.

They both froze, waiting and listening.

Apparently, Jake expected some loud bumps as his toy hauler crossed the rough desert ground because he didn't stop, even though he couldn't have missed the noise. Cal and Drina bounced and banged for what seemed like hours but was probably only twenty minutes or so. At last Jake pulled onto a fairly smooth dirt road for another few miles before they hit asphalt and the ride smoothed out even more.

Cal rose and slid into the booth, his movements slow and careful. He eased the curtain slightly open and looked out, then slapped it shut.

"What is it?"

He slid down beside her to whisper. "We're passing the tollbooth where we stopped last night. Carter's black SUV is parked by the stream's edge."

"Did you see him?"

"No. No one's in sight, thankfully, or they might have seen me moving the curtain. I guarantee there'll be another vehicle parked at the intersection of the road and the highway."

The road curved again, and Drina slid to

the side of the booth. She winced and one hand flew to the other arm. Relenting, Cal held her steady with an arm around her shoulder. He tried not to notice how snugly she fit next to him, like she belonged there.

"The motion will ease up once we hit the highway." *And as soon as it does, you're going back to your side of the bench.*

"Do you have any idea where we're headed?"

He shook his head. "Not a clue, but anywhere away from here is good."

"I had my heart set on reaching the base this afternoon. It's not going to happen, is it?"

Cal said nothing and Drina's whole body sagged in disappointment. She looked so sad and defeated. The need to comfort her was winning Cal's internal battle.

The trailer slowed and once again, she tensed. Cal grasped her hand and squeezed. "Relax. We've just come to the 'T' of the highway intersection. He can only go right or left."

"Which way is the base?"

Cal paused, waiting. The truck geared up and the trailer swayed left. Cal sagged just a little. "We're headed to the mountains. Lake Isabella, to be precise."

"But you said we didn't want to go there."

"That was before our quad was washed

away. Since we're on foot now, they'll expect us to make our way to the nearest help."

"That means the people in the campground."

"Right. But no one knows we were there. No one will be in danger."

"Except us. We need help."

He shook his head. "Isabella is good. They won't be looking for us there. Sit back. Try to relax. There is only one place we can go once he turns left—Kernville. It's at least a two-hour drive away."

Drina closed her eyes and leaned back against the soft cushion of the booth. She looked bone weary, cold and in pain. Just then her stomach grumbled. Sighing, she opened her eyes.

"Cal, do you suppose…" She couldn't even finish her sentence. She just pointed to the small refrigerator under the counter.

He leaned forward. "I should have thought of that." He scooted across the floor and loosened the latch on the small appliance. Inside were string cheese, apples, a package of raw hamburger and a whole shelf of bottled water.

Cal popped the lid on one and handed it to Drina. She poured it down her throat.

As she gulped the last of it, Cal handed her another. "I'm afraid this has to be the last. I don't think he'll miss a bottle or two but we don't want to take so much that he'll notice and wonder if someone's been here."

He handed her a wrapper of string cheese, then pulled a discarded plastic bag out of a trash can under the booth's table. "We'll pack out our trash, too."

She nodded, then ate the cheese. Cal handed her an apple.

When they finished, he wrapped all their trash in the bag, and then pointed to the computer still clutched in her hands.

"Don't you want to set that down and get more comfortable?"

She shook her head and pulled it closer. "I don't want another experience like the one in the riverbed when I left it behind."

He didn't want that, either. In fact, he didn't think his embattled senses could take another scare like that. "Suit yourself. But you'll want to sleep while you can."

"That won't be a problem. With the hunger pangs in my stomach eased, I'm already halfway there." Her eyelids drooped and her head tilted to the side. Pink lips parted. Her breathing eased and she leaned into Cal. He hesitated, but after a few moments he looped his arm over and pulled her close. He wasn't sure but he thought a small smile lifted the corners of her mouth.

That smile melted something hard inside him, something steel-like. But he couldn't let his determination dissolve. He absolutely had to stay focused on finding the identity of the boss. Too many people were counting on him to complete his mission…and Drina Gallagher had the potential to be as dangerous to that goal as the men chasing them.

FOUR

"Come on, Drina. Time to move."

Drina opened her eyes and scrambled to look out the window.

Still groggy, she rolled to her knees and tried to rise. Every muscle in her body screamed and she almost collapsed flat on her face.

The trailer door flipped open and Cal came back, lifting her to her feet and pointing her to the door. A blast of freezing air stole her breath and she gasped.

"We're at a higher elevation here in the mountains. We'll have to find you something warmer to wear."

They stood in the parking lot of a business. The trailer blocked their view of the building behind, but the sign in front said Sharkey's Auto Repair. Across the busy main street, a community park sprawled over a couple of acres.

"Let's go." Cal took her arm and marched her toward the sidewalk. Drina almost stepped off the curb to cross the street, but Cal's firm hold on her arm stopped her. He turned her toward the corner.

"No jaywalking. We don't want to attract attention."

Drina nodded numbly and leaned into him. *Thank You. Thank You for Cal. I don't know where I'd be without him.*

Yes, I do know where I'd be. Dead.

That sobering thought jolted Drina's exhausted mind fully awake. She straightened and looked around. Just down the street, advertisements for sports equipment and white-water-rapids trips filled a portion of a store window.

"Do you think we could buy a coat there?"

"A coat and other things." He patted his pocket.

As they moved forward, a thought came to her. "Where did you get all that cash?"

"From my account. The boss deposited it the night of your kidnapping."

"He has access to your account?"

"We have a joint account under a couple of aliases where he deposits my pay. Usually I withdraw the money as soon as he pays me and put it in my own account. The agency once tried leaving it in the account so we could trace the originating location. But the boss routes the money through too many banks and switches them all the time." He shook his head. "I knew something was up that night he told me to withdraw the money and bring it to the meeting place. I just didn't realize he intended to leave it behind as a ploy to implicate you."

"Who would have thought he'd drop twenty thousand dollars just to implicate a dead woman."

"That's the point, Drina. They'll make billions off your plans. Twenty thousand is just a drop in the bucket."

And that's why I'll never let them get their hands on my computer.

She didn't say the words out loud. Cal had already expressed his opinion on the value of her work. He wouldn't understand her desperate compulsion to keep it safe, because he considered her life more important. She wasn't sure she understood it herself. Why risk her life and, worse, Cal's? Was her work more important than his life?

A day ago she would have said yes. But not now. Why? What had changed?

Nothing. Just because a handsome stranger tumbled into her life on the edge of a storm—

a stranger who was thoughtful and amazing—did that mean everything she'd worked for should go out the door? Isn't that what happened with John?

She'd lost her head and focus. Let her emotions control her actions, and a wonderful, vibrant man had ended up dead. She couldn't let that happen again. She wouldn't. No matter how enigmatic and attractive Cal was, she had to stay focused on getting her work into safe hands. Opening herself up…letting herself feel would only end badly, just like it had with John.

Her parents had been right all those years ago. Her romantic inclinations were not to be trusted.

Cal opened the glass door to the sporting goods store and held it for Drina, who stopped short as she caught her reflection and sighed. His gaze followed hers, over her bobbed hair, still shiny in spite of all she'd been through. She bent and tried to brush dirt from her still-damp jeans.

"I'm a mess. I look like I've been through a war."

"You have been," Cal murmured as she passed under his arm and through the door. "And for the record, I think you look great."

Drina made a rude little sound. "Right."

Cal didn't miss the heavy sarcasm in her tone as she marched straight toward a rack of down-filled jackets.

In two strides he caught up to her and grasped her arm. "I mean what I say, Drina. I don't pay people false compliments."

His words seemed to tickle her funny bone. Chuckling, she looked around then leaned in to whisper, "This from the man who's been undercover for two years. Your whole life is false."

She chuckled again. Her hazel eyes sparkled. Cal wanted to just stand there and admire them.

"Okay. Point taken." Her smile eased his spirit, made his tone lighten. "But I meant everything I said." He allowed his gaze to travel over her once more. "Even in the middle of that storm with the wind whipping all around your face, your hair looked great."

"It's trying to frizz."

He shook his head and lowered his gaze as if speaking to a naughty child. "It's like black silk and lays in waves. The way it sets against your skin…you have this amazing skin. And why you hide your eyes behind those big black Mr. Peabody glasses is a mystery to me."

"Um…maybe because I need to read…?"

That smile flashed again and Cal's stomach did a flip-flop. "Make as many jokes as you want, Drina, but I know women who would kill for your looks."

His compliments seemed to make her uncomfortable. She even tried to divert his attention away with words that just seemed to pop out.

"You're one to talk. You have this one piece of black hair that falls over your forehead just like Superman. Not to mention a smile that makes you more lethal than that gun you carry."

She snapped her lips shut and her eyes widened as if she was as surprised at her words as he was.

The words and her reaction brought a bona fide grin to his lips. "Why, Drina Gallagher! You do like me." He stepped a little closer and his tone dropped to a murmur.

She seemed at a loss for words. The brainchild was flummoxed. Cal had scored a point and his grin broadened.

"May I help you?" The interruption stopped Drina from replying. Much to Cal's chagrin… he was fairly certain she was about to deny their attraction. He would have liked to drive home his point, maybe pierce that wall Ms.

Gallagher kept around herself. Maybe then he could figure out what she was thinking and straighten out his own muddled thoughts, as well.

Unfortunately, the clerk stood right beside them. Her gaze traveled up and down their disheveled appearance, a frown creasing her forehead.

Smooth as silk, Cal wrapped an arm around Drina and pulled her to his side. "Actually, you can. My wife and I are renting a cabin for our very first vacation together. We didn't even have a honeymoon."

He smiled again. "We had an accident on the way up here. Our car was rear-ended… just enough damage to jam our trunk. It'll be another day before they can get our luggage out so we need a few things to get us through."

Cal's quick explanation seemed to ease the clerk's concerns. "I'm so sorry to hear that. How can I help?"

"My wife can pick out some clothing, so if you'll lead me to the backpacking equipment, I'll look for some toothbrushes and sundries. We want to keep everything lightweight and portable. We're avid backpackers. That's why we're here…scouting out the area for some summer trips."

"Oh, then you'll definitely want to take a look at our white-water trips. We have some great packages."

She led Cal in the opposite direction. He glanced back at Drina and winked. His reward was another shake of her head, but he knew he'd flustered her again. Good. That made two of them.

The clerk led him to a wall of sundry items small enough to fit in a new backpack. Cal thanked her and sorted through them, keeping an eye on the door and Drina at the same time. He'd purposely teased her to lighten the mood, hoping to pierce that wall. He wanted…needed to know, to understand, to piece together the puzzle of Drina and why she ignited such conflicting feelings in him. Then maybe he could forget about the petite, enigmatic engineer and concentrate on salvaging his mission.

He looked back to see her piling warm gloves, socks, dry tennis shoes, a thermal shirt and hiking pants in her arms. For good measure, she found a sweatshirt and pants and threw them on the pile. She walked toward him, her arms overflowing.

"I think I'm ready."

He pointed toward the checkout stand. She stacked her clothes on the counter and took off the jacket. As the clerk rang up their order, Drina added two boxes of protein and energy bars to the purchase.

Cal quirked an eyebrow in her direction but said nothing. He simply pulled out five hundred-dollar bills. The clerk counted out his change. Drina put the parka on and popped the gloves out of the wrapping before handing the trash to the obviously impressed clerk. Cal took the bags and on the way to the door, Drina peeled back the wrapper on one of the protein bars.

Outside, Cal's lips lifted in a wry twist. "You seem to be enjoying yourself."

"I am." She took a big bite of nuts and dried fruit. "It's always nice to spend someone else's money...especially someone you don't like."

Cal laughed out loud. "I kind of felt the same way."

He dug out a bottle of water. "I'd love to stop and grab something hot to drink, but we have quite a hike ahead of us."

"Where are we going?"

"To a cabin about five miles up the mountain."

She tossed the bar's wrapper in a trash can along the sidewalk. "I suppose you're going to use that little tool in your pocket to pick the lock again."

He handed her the bottle. "Don't need to. I have a key."

Drina held up a finger in an unspoken gesture to wait as she swallowed half the bottle of water he'd handed her.

"I don't think I'll ever quench my thirst. How do you have a key and how do you know so much about the area? When we were in Red Rock Canyon, you even knew the back roads."

"I've been out here for two years, Drina. I've done a lot of scouting. It's my job to know the area, to search for possible escape routes and to cover my tracks. I have a key to that cabin because it's mine. I bought it under an alias and set it up as a safe house."

"How safe *is* your safe house?"

"It's good enough. It's not connected to my life on base and no one knows about it. I visit it every other month and keep it stocked with food, money, medical supplies and weapons. It's a place where I can hide…and sometimes where I can just be myself."

She stopped in the middle of the sidewalk. "If it's so safe, why don't we just call your contacts and hole up there until they arrive?"

He sighed and stepped back. Linking his

fingers with her gloved ones, he pulled her forward. "We don't know who we can trust, remember? Besides, if I can stop dodging bullets long enough to think, I might be able to find a way to trap the boss."

He turned up the walk again, his hand firmly latched with hers. He liked the feel of her dainty hand in his. He needed to let go, needed to focus on his mission, but he didn't release her even when she followed along docilely.

They reached the edge of town and turned off the main street heading up the mountain, deeper into the forest. Buildings and homes disappeared from view down long, twisting drives. The sounds of busy traffic on the main street faded. The clear, clean scent of pine filled the air. Bright morning sun lent a sparkle to the soft dusting of snow on the pine branches and bushes. Birds twittered close by and in the distance, the soft *tap-tap-tap* of a woodpecker replaced the rumble of engines.

Suddenly, Drina halted in her footsteps. "It's good to be alive." She turned to Cal and her green-tinted gaze met his. "Thank you for saving my life."

He gripped her fingers. "You are most welcome, Drina Gallagher." With that he tugged her forward.

They walked on and Drina seemed to be wrapped in a soft glow. But the glow faded as one mile turned into two. They climbed and climbed. Drina asked fifteen times how much farther.

"It has to be secluded to be safe. Just a little while longer."

"You sound so patient. How can you be when all I want to do is yell at you for not stopping at the closest hotel on the main strip? I would have even tolerated one of those nasty, hundred-year-old motor hotels if the bed had a blanket."

Wisely, Cal kept his mouth shut. Obviously, the strength she'd gained from her two-hour rest in the back of Jake's trailer was depleted.

"My feet hurt. If we walk one more mile, I'm going to lie down on the next pile of pine needles and sleep."

"No need. This is my lane."

"It's a dirt road."

Cal gestured. "Look there. You'll see my log cabin."

Glimpses of his safe house appeared through the pine trees. From a distance, the logs looked old and rustic, but it was an illusion. Cal had retrofitted the windows and doors. They were modern, tight…and warm… which sounded appealing to him, too.

Three wide steps led to a porch the width of the cabin. Cal lunged up but Drina stood, wavering like someone drunk.

He pulled up a board on the porch and retrieved the key from a small box hidden below, then unlocked and pushed the door open. But he had to go back down the stairs and lift Drina.

He carried her into the cabin, shut the door and bolted it. At the flip of a switch, golden light filled the room. Everything was just as he'd left it. The large rock fireplace across the room. A leather couch with a rust-colored throw draped over the back. To the right, the kitchen and a hall leading to the bedrooms.

Drina started for the couch, but Cal grasped her elbow and led her to the spare bedroom. He flipped a switch and light flooded the semidark room, revealing a large bed under a patchwork quilt.

"Take off those damp clothes and get into bed. I'll see if I can't get the heat going."

He didn't need to say it twice. With fumbling fingers she stripped off her gloves and unzipped the parka. Dropping it on the floor, she worked the zipper of her other jacket. Beneath, she wore a gray, form-fitting flannel T-shirt.

Cal turned away. Now that they were safe,

he needed to make all thoughts of Drina Gallagher off-limits.

She was dangerous. Top secret information flowed through her like water through a sieve. Not to mention the fact that her intense but misguided loyalties had already put both their lives in danger and almost certainly destroyed his hopes of breaking the spy ring. Buddy deserved better.

Cal shut the door with a little more force than necessary.

Drina's eyes scratched like sandpaper as she opened them. For a moment or two she couldn't remember where she was. Simple log walls. A small oak desk. A bed stand with a brass lamp. She turned to look around and every muscle in her body screamed. Slumping back against the pillow, she lay still...until the scent of something wonderful drifted to her nose, buried beneath the heavy quilt.

Food. Good food.

Her stomach protested so loudly she had to move. Throwing back the covers, she pushed the computer farther beneath the blankets. Sometime in her half-dead state, she'd pulled it off the floor and stuffed it beneath her pillow. Amazed that she'd had that much sense, she steeled herself against the complaints of her weary body and sat on the edge of the bed. She was dying of thirst. She needed a bathroom, water and food, in that order. Everything else could wait.

To her right, a bathroom offered a tiny shower. That, too, could wait, even though the zip tie cuts on her wrists hurt like crazy and might have been infected. Splashing water on her face, she fingered her hair, slipped into the sweats Cal had purchased with the boss's money and headed toward the wonderful scent.

Spaghetti? Sautéed onions and garlic. Definitely marinara.

She opened the small bedroom door and heard the soft strains of classical music. A fire roared in the large river-rock fireplace. Across the room, a wide, double-paned window revealed soft white flakes falling in the twilight.

"It's snowing." She spoke out loud without thinking.

"Ahhh…the sleeping beauty awakes."

Cal stood behind the kitchen island/breakfast bar, stirring a large pot on the stove.

"Barely. I could probably sleep more. Judging from the dusky light out there I've only been asleep for a few hours. Is it late afternoon?"

Cal paused and leaned against the counter with both hands, palms flat. "Yes. It is. Twenty-four hours later."

Drina stopped. "Twenty-four hours?"

"That's right. You've slept around the clock. I put in a good fourteen hours myself, but you were down for the count. I was considering checking on you just to make sure you were still breathing. But then I thought if my marinara didn't wake you, nothing would." He gestured to the pot.

"Your marinara? Did you make it from scratch?"

"Yep."

"It smells wonderful and I'm starving."

"It'll be ready in about half an hour." Crossing to the fridge, he pulled out a bottle of water. "I suggest you start hydrating now."

"Thanks. I'm really thirsty." She took the bottle and twisted it open as she moved toward the window and the snowy scene in front of her.

"Is this the tail end of the storm that caused the flash flood?"

"Actually, it's a blessing from God."

She hated it when he used phrases like that. In her experience God didn't bestow blessings. He just took things away. Frowning, she looked over her shoulder. "What's that supposed to mean?"

"It means we're getting a break. This is a brand-new storm, a doozy, trailing right behind the other one. They're expecting record snowfall, maybe even a blizzard. All the airports are shut down and probably the roads."

"Shut down the roads? How is that a blessing? Now we can't get to the base."

"God's giving us a reprieve, Drina. If we can't get out, the bad guys can't get in. We desperately needed rest and food. This storm will give us that plus time to move cautiously and plan. Perhaps I can come up with a way to get you to safety and still salvage my mission."

"You said that yesterday. It didn't make sense then and it doesn't make sense now."

Behind her, Cal said nothing. The silence stretched on until Drina couldn't bear it. She looked back again. His gaze was fixed on her with a frown that made her cringe inside.

"Have you considered what will happen after that? We don't know where the leak is, Drina. You've risked your life to keep the plans safe. You'll take them back, maybe even build the weapon, and in six months, when it's operational, the mole will leak the plans and everything you've risked will have been for nothing."

She hadn't thought that far ahead…hadn't

had the chance. Now that Cal put the possibility into such simple terms, the scenario chilled her.

She shivered and rubbed her free hand up and down her arm. "I just need to get the plans to Bill. I trust him completely. He'll know what to do."

"I'm not so sure."

She spun. "What do you mean?"

Cal snipped the end off a package of pasta and slid the contents into a pot of boiling water. "I've been going over the events of your kidnapping in my head. I don't think the informer is on my end."

Another cold shiver rippled over Drina. "So just like that, my company is at fault."

"Think about it, Drina. I went into that meeting at the wind farm cold turkey. I had a gut feeling that you might be there but no other indication. Don't you think something would have changed in my chain of information if the informant was on my side? I didn't even get your phone message in time to respond. Yet Carter and Whitson picked you up minutes after you made that call to me. Tell me what you did to alert them."

She took a deep breath. "I called Bill's home phone and told him I'd solved the problem."

"You called Bill on an unsecured line?"

Nodding, she hung her head. "I was so excited… I just didn't think. But Bill stopped me from saying too much. He told me to hang up and send the equations I'd discovered on the company's secured email."

"Then what happened?"

"I wrote the plans out. Typed them in a coherent order and prepared to attach the file to an email."

"Prepared? You didn't send them?"

The truth hit her even as he asked the question. "I got cold feet. I remembered part of your security briefing about eyes and ears. I couldn't trust…"

Cal leaned forward on the counter again. "Deep down you felt something wasn't right in your own company."

She nodded with grim acknowledgment. "So I kept the information to myself, just to make sure I'd *have* to be kidnapped." Her tone perfectly portrayed her disgust with her decision.

"Don't be too hard on yourself. You had no way of knowing all of our security measures would fail. It's a reflection of how good these people are. It's taken me two years to even get this close."

He shook his head. "What disturbs me most is how quickly they acted. Not ten minutes after your conversation with Bill, Carter and Whitson were on location, ready to snatch you."

"Whoever the boss is has to be close to Bill."

"And close enough to you to know your workaholic habits. You never work from home. You usually stay at the lab long after everyone else is gone."

Her lips twisted in a slight smile. "You know my habits and we're not that close."

"I told you. I know more about you than you think."

His lips lifted in a slight smile that made her stomach jump. That crazy little jump was followed by a very loud grumble.

All the way across the room Cal smiled. "You need food. This is almost ready. Have a seat and I'll give you a roll hot out of the oven."

Drina didn't need a second invitation. She hurried over and settled onto a colonial-style chair situated beneath a simple plank table—polished to a sheen, yet rustic and masculine, like the rest of the cabin. A dark leather couch. Maple trestle-style end tables. The cross section of a pine tree, finished and mounted on tree-trunk legs, for a coffee table.

Simple, tasteful and with the large, roaring fire, cozy in a rustic way.

The tantalizing aroma of the fresh rolls Cal set in front of her added to the homey feel of his cabin. The bread was almost too hot to touch but that didn't stop Drina. She grabbed a roll and tossed it from one hand to the other, helping it to cool before she scooped off a slab of fresh butter.

"Real butter. Homemade rolls. How did you manage all this?" Steam rolled off the freshly opened bread and she closed her eyes as she inhaled the yeasty scent.

"I can store flour and sugar, basic ingredients in plastic containers and they last much better than packaged products. Whenever I'm here, I fill the freezer and restock my basics just for an occasion like this. It is a safe house, after all."

"A safe haven." Drina spoke around a mouthful of roll. She didn't know if her hunger made the bread tastier but it melted in her mouth as easily as the butter. She reached for another just as Cal set a bowl of spaghetti covered in marinara sauce in front of her. The sweet, tangy scent of the sauce drifted upward and her stomach gave another gurgle.

Grabbing her fork, she wound the pasta around and around the tines, then helped herself to the most perfect bite of spaghetti she'd ever sampled. She took another bite and another. Cal sat down across from her with his own plate.

Smiling, he ducked his head. "I take it you like it."

With her mouth full, Drina could only nod.

"Good." Cal dived into his own food, the smile lingering on his lips.

They ate in silence. As Drina finished her second helping and dabbed her lips with a napkin, Cal clasped his hands and leaned them on the table.

"I'd like to say a prayer of thanksgiving if you don't mind."

Her fingers flew to her lips. She may not agree with Cal's Christian faith but she didn't want to get in the way of it. "I'm sorry. Of course you did. You probably wanted to pray before we ate."

He gave another shake of his head and his lips twisted into the wry smile Drina was beginning to recognize. "In the last forty-eight hours you've had a granola bar and half a bottle of water. I think the Lord will understand your haste."

He bowed his head. "Heavenly Father, we thank You for bringing us through the desert safely. For protecting us and guiding us.

I thank You for sending me to that shack in time and keeping my aim clear and true."

Yes, thank You for sending this man.

"I also thank You for Drina and her courage in saving my life and I pray for the soul of Whitson, wherever he may be."

Startled, Drina looked up to study Cal's bowed head. What a complex man he was. Cool, collected and calculating when in danger. Filled with compassion and yes…remorse, later.

He glanced up and saw her watching him. For the first time, his gaze darted away from hers.

Why was he suddenly uncomfortable? Was he sorry she had witnessed his regret? Was he embarrassed? Did he think it made him seem weak?

Drina didn't see it that way. His sincere compassion made him one of the most compelling men she'd ever met. Suddenly, she wanted to know more about him…she wanted to know *all* about him. But he rose from the table, forestalling any questions.

Drina rose, too, and began to gather her dishes. Cal grasped her hand, stilling her movement. His hand was warm and firm and so very, very comforting. Once again, his touch felt like a lifeline she never wanted to release.

"I'll take care of the dishes." He lifted her hand and turned it over, exposing the red, inflamed cuts on her wrist. "What I'd like you to do is take care of these."

He ran a finger along her wrist near the cuts. The simple gesture sent warmth shooting through her.

"I—I would like to take a shower."

"I have a better idea. Come with me."

He linked his fingers through hers and led her toward his bedroom—which was almost as large as the living area. A king-size bed covered in a huge quilt of browns and beiges dominated the space. To the left, French doors opened to a meadow, revealing gently falling, oversize snowflakes. To the right, a bathroom…and tucked into a corner of the spacious area was a large bathtub, framed by wood and built up with river rock.

"Is that a spa?"

"It's a spa tub with air jets."

Candles rested on one corner of the redwood decking. Two fluffy white towels draped over the other corner. Just to the side of the tub, a sink nestled into a wood vanity.

Cal pulled a toothbrush package, a small travel-size tube of toothpaste and bottles of shampoo and conditioner out of a drawer and set them on the sink.

"Do you have everything in this cabin?"

"Everything I think I might need," he said with a nod. "It *is* a safe house."

He pulled matches out of the drawer and lit the candles. Then he showed her how to work the faucets and the aerator for maximum relief.

"And this…" He held up a small jar of what looked like purple crystals. "This is the secret ingredient. Epsom salts. Good for sore muscles and minor cuts. It's also scented like pines for maximum relaxation."

Drina laughed. "I can't believe you'd have something quite so feminine-looking in your cabin."

He grinned, a full-fledged smile that made Drina's heart do some kind of flip-flop thing again. Her gaze lingered. She loved that very becoming dimple in his right cheek.

"There's nothing feminine about these Epsom salts. I have a rigorous workout routine that leaves me with as many muscle aches and pains as you're experiencing right now. One soak in these babies and I'm good as new. So fill the tub, sit back and relax."

He turned down the overhead lights and shut the door behind her.

Drina stepped up to the tub and started the water, making it extra hot. She brushed her teeth as it filled. When steam rolled over the tub, she poured in a generous scoop of Cal's salts…and an extra pinch for good measure.

FIVE

By the time Drina wiped down the tub and dropped the towels in a rattan basket, her legs felt like jelly. She hadn't been this relaxed in…well…years.

Had her life really become so complicated, so driven, so…judgmental?

As long as she could remember she'd adhered to her parents' theory that narrow-minded fanaticism focused on one thing at the cost of all logical thought. That was why she'd always felt John's death, born of misguided patriotism, was such a disastrous waste of a good man.

But Cal made her see things differently. With him, duty didn't come before others. It came *because* of others. He'd sacrificed his mission to save her life. His saw his duty as protecting others and even risked his life to do it. And obviously she needed protecting. She'd made a mess of her situation.

They seemed to have the same goals, so why did she fight Cal every step of the way? Even when he was saving her life?

There had to be some other reason, some underlying motive she couldn't see. But she was too tired to think about it now. She was relaxed and ready for another marathon sleep, but a tantalizing smell compelled her to investigate. Fingering her damp bob into place, she headed out.

As soon as she entered the front room the sweet aroma swept over her like a tidal wave.

"Chocolate. You're luring me into your web with chocolate."

"Mexican hot chocolate to be exact." Cal crossed the room with two mugs in hand. "I'm making sure I get plenty of liquids in you while I can. But I have to be inventive with only powdered milk in the house."

Drina plopped onto the leather couch and blew on the steaming drink. One sip later she closed her eyes in pure bliss. "How do you do this? Where did you learn to cook?"

Cal eased back on the couch and placed one long, lean ankle on his knee. "My mother. She's a gourmet cook and was one of the head chefs at a popular San Diego restaurant for years. She was always in the kitchen experimenting, trying new dishes and I was right beside her."

A sweet smile slipped over his lips. "We had a big, open family room and kitchen setup, like this. My mom and I would be in the kitchen, cookin' away, and my dad and my sister would be in the family room, rockin' out."

"Rockin' out?"

"My dad was a high school music teacher and a jazz musician. My sister loved to do the vocals. In fact, she still does. She makes pretty good money as a studio singer."

Drina suppressed a shiver. "Cooking. Jazz and singing. Your house must have oozed creativity."

Cal laughed. "Is that such a bad thing?"

Drina paused. "Not bad. I just wouldn't know what to do surrounded by all that."

Cal pinned his blue gaze on her. Why had she not noticed how the blue in his eyes was a light shade? That light blue accounted for the gray cast. She didn't think she'd ever seen eyes quite that color.

She was definitely relaxed. She never had these romanticized ideas…nor was she this talkative…especially about her family. But somehow, here in Cal's presence, in this house, everything really did seem "safe."

"What were you surrounded with?"

"Numbers. Classes. Studies."

"Are you telling me your parents never relaxed?"

"That is relaxing to them. They have very active minds so they keep busy. Don't get me wrong, they have active social lives, too. They are both heads of committees and brain trusts. They travel to conferences a lot. I have to say I probably knew my way around a hotel better than most adults."

"Travel is good. You probably saw a lot."

Drina's relaxed eyes drooped shut and she laughed. "Sure. Just about everything there was to see from a hotel window."

Did she mean for her tone to be so bitter? Was she really that resentful? She'd struggled for so long to be a part of her parents' world—a world of the nation's top minds. Why, then, did she make her childhood sound so empty? She rushed to defend her past.

"They had dinner parties with very important people whenever they were home. I met some individuals who shaped our lives…the world. They'd have these long, lengthy discussions after dinner and my parents would let me listen in."

Her eyes closed again as visions and memories drifted through her mind.

"Sounds like every kid's idea of a fun night."

Sarcasm was heavy in his tone. It caused Drina's hackles to rise. But only slightly. She was too relaxed, too tired for much else.

"It was *my* idea of a great night. You can't imagine what it was like to listen to the great thinkers of our time. To hear their thoughts and disappointments, even their hopes for the future. Listening to them, I felt like nothing was impossible. I wanted to be like them, to help shape the future, to change the world." Her gaze shifted to the crackling fire, her mind caught up once more in memories.

"Sounds like a really big goal for such a little girl."

She giggled, sounding girlish even to her own ears. "It was. But I did it."

"Well, you should be pleased. Your work is a great accomplishment."

As the fire crackled, she shook her head. "Somehow my grandiose vision of the future didn't involve running for my life through the desert."

"Don't do that."

Cal's tone was firm, causing her to raise her gaze from the flames.

"Don't try to shoulder all the blame."

She twisted her head on the couch so she

could look at him fully. "Not so long ago you were perfectly fine with blaming me."

One dark eyebrow quirked. "It's true that you made foolish mistakes. But you are no more responsible for these men's despicable actions than you were for John's choices. He had free will. He volunteered for his own purposes and maybe even sacrificed his own life to save others, his fellow soldiers. Maybe even died protecting civilians…women and children. Whatever happened, let John's choices be his and yours be yours. And most important, don't let these men's evil destroy your hope."

Once again she was struck by the force of his words. This man exuded power in his actions and his thoughts. He was a force to be reckoned with and that force came in such a pretty package. It was easy to have hope when she looked into his eyes. He made her feel that all was right with the world. He possessed heartfelt confidence. A steel jaw. Nice firm lips. One dark lock falling over his forehead.

Superman.

She felt like he could make everything right. And right now Drina wanted Superman to lean over and kiss her. She needed some of his strength, some of his hope and she wanted it to come with the feel of his arms around her.

"You shouldn't look at me like that," he murmured.

"Like what?" Was that truly her voice sounding so…so flirtatious?

"Like you want me to kiss you. If you keep doing that, I will."

"Would that be so bad?"

One side of his mouth lifted in a quirk of a smile and Drina longed to place her lips right on that crazy little tilted corner.

"Not for me, it wouldn't." His voice was low, so low it vibrated through her. "I'd be very happy to kiss you. But I suspect once you weren't so loopy from exhaustion, you might take exception to my kiss. You'd probably wake up in the morning and want my head on a platter."

"Such a nice head it is, too." She smiled.

Cal gave a little laugh and rose. Reaching down, he tugged her to her feet. "Come on. Let's get you to bed before I do something you'll regret."

As he pulled her down the hall, she followed, stumbling over her own feet. All the way and even after she'd climbed into bed, her mind turned his twisted phrase over and over. Superman wanted to kiss her…as much as she wanted to kiss him. Maybe even more. The thought made her smile.

She started to drift off, an image of Cal's dimple floating through her mind. He reminded her of John. That thought made the smile fade.

In fact, Cal was exactly like John. A devout Christian. Patriotic. Determined to do his duty even to the point of sacrificing his own life.

What was it with her? Why was she attracted to men with hero complexes?

Wide awake now, she stared into the shadows of the dark room. She already felt responsible for the death of one man. The last thing she wanted was to put another one in harm's way. Because no matter how much Cal made her feel like he was a superman, speeding bullets *would* stop him.

He'd already placed himself between Drina and danger. She couldn't let it happen again. One way or another, they had to get to safety before he tried to save her one too many times.

Cal leaned back in his chair to study the two side-by-side folders in front of him. He'd desperately needed sleep and food to think clearly…as well as a break from Drina's constant presence. Her very nearness was wreaking havoc on his professionalism and he couldn't let that happen. His team was counting on him. So he'd stopped running and slept.

But he'd put off contacting his home base too long, so he rose early and pulled out his files, determined to find some answers. Truth be told he knew they'd want to pull the plug on the operation and he wanted—needed—to see if he could salvage the work before he let them.

He'd spent hours going over every suspect he'd collected through the years, eliminating and cross-checking each person, comparing positions, access to information and liabilities. Only two men met all of his criteria. One of them had to be the boss.

Hal Jacobi was the head engineer of all test projects on Edwards Air Force Base, including Drina's program. He was a well-respected civilian employee and engineer. He'd worked at the base for years, knew everyone and everything important enough to know. Plus, he had access to all the programs that had been compromised. He also supervised a high-level engineer with a serious gambling debt. Jacobi's failure to report his employee's debt to Cal's base security team was a major breach.

Gambling debts, affairs, secrets of any kind posed threats. Any weakness could be used against an employee to extort information. For Jacobi not to report the engineer—a programmer with access to Drina's project—was a serious mistake and a red flag for Cal. So why had Jacobi held back the info?

Cal's team would have placed a watch on the engineer, nothing more serious. So why did Jacobi not report him? Was he covering for his employee…or blackmailing him to feed Jacobi info? What was the answer?

Cal's second suspect was Bill Carlisle, Drina's supervisor at Aero Electronics, a private corporation that ran most of their tests on the base. Carlisle and Jacobi had inside info and direct lines to all the projects that had been compromised. In Cal's book that made them both suspects.

However, unlike Jacobi, Carlisle had a spotless record. No red flags. No culpable employees, and more important, by the time Cal had reached the site where Drina had been kidnapped, Carlisle had reported Drina's security misstep to the military police and sent them to check on her. And what about the connection Drina had heard on Carlisle's phone? The man certainly hadn't wiretapped his own phone.

Still, Cal couldn't shake the feeling that something wasn't right. Carlisle triggered his senses into high alert. But Cal couldn't seem to pinpoint a reason, and instincts weren't evidence.

Jacobi seemed to be Cal's most likely suspect. But how could he prove it? How could he catch the man now that his cover was blown?

His only contact with the organization had been through his mysterious phone man. Every attempt to trace the calls ended at a blank wall. The man purchased throwaway phones each time and used an instrument to alter his voice.

Carter and Whitson had been his only face-to-face contacts. Going five years back, neither man had associations with anyone remotely connected to Aero Electronics, the military or any of the individuals involved in the programs. In fact, neither man had a record at all. They'd appeared out of nowhere with new identities and backgrounds that started five years ago.

Cal's efforts brought him back to his one clue. The tap on Carlisle's phone. Who had been listening in on the conversation between Carlisle and Drina?

Now was the time for answers. He turned

on his computer and connected to his email.
Here, in his safe house, he had direct contact
with his team in Washington. Even with the
bad weather, he might still be able to connect
via his satellite connection. He plunked out
the email address and waited. After a delay
that had him giving up hope, the server finally connected.

Cal breathed with relief. His handler, Harris, came on the line immediately.

I'm glad to hear from you. I've had a sinking feeling ever since you went dark. I have a
suspicion that Gallagher's disappearance has
something to do with your message. Did you
locate her? Is she alive?

Yes. I have her, but my cover is blown.

Then the operation is over.

Need more info before we call it. Did the re-
quest I made for the tapping of Jacobi and
Carlisle's phones go into effect?

Yes.

When did the tapping start?

Not sure. I'll need to validate.

Do it quickly and get back to me. Drina heard someone on Carlisle's line the night she called him. I think it might have been our tap.

Is it safe to wait for the confirmation? Do you and the girl need to be extracted?

Cal's fingers paused over the keys. By all rights, he should call for extraction and get Drina to safety. But still...he hesitated.

We're in my safe house. Good for now. Get me that information and then we'll make the call.

Will do.

Harris clicked off, and Cal shut down the program, hoping he hadn't just made a mistake. But they were temporarily safe and he needed more time. He was convinced Drina held the clue to the man's identity. She was closest to the project. Something she had heard or seen might be the info Cal needed. It may not have seemed important to her at the time, but he had to go over the events with her again, just to be sure.

He absolutely could not give up on his mission yet, and he had the feeling that if he and Drina were safely tucked away at CIA headquarters, the boss and his cohorts would disappear…this time for good. He couldn't fail again. Buddy and all the boss's victims deserved better.

Hearing Drina stir in the bedroom, he grabbed the files and headed out to the kitchen. Drina came in a few moments later, walking slowly, the hood of her sweatshirt pulled over her head. She winced every time she took a step and that told Cal all he needed to know.

"Sore?" He handed her a cup of coffee, black and strong.

"I can barely move." Her tone was just above a murmur as if even talking hurt.

"The first couple of days after an event are usually the worst."

Wrapping her fingers around the mug, she trudged to the window, slowly making her way across the living room. Cal couldn't stop the small chuckle that slipped out.

"It's not funny," she mumbled as she passed him.

"No. It's not. I'm sorry, but if you could see the way you're walking…"

A light dusting of snow floated across their view through the window. Glancing back—

without moving too much—she said, "It looks like the weather report was wrong. This was no blizzard."

Cal shook his head. "This is the lull before the real storm hits. Minutes ago the wind was whipping the snow in a flurry. Airports and roads are closed in and out. Usually, I drive my SUV so I have it if necessary. I tuck it in the garage where no one will see it. Everyone here associates me with a small economy car. There's very little crossover from my life on the base and my life here. But I don't have my SUV this time and my economy car wouldn't make it down the road let alone off the mountain. Fortunately for us, no cars can make it in right now, either, so we're safe...for a short while."

She didn't say more. He wondered if she remembered much of what she'd said last night. Little indications, like her dropped glance and reluctance to meet his gaze, confirmed his decision. If he *had* followed his inclinations and kissed her, his head would be on a plate today.

Not for the first time, Cal wondered how thick those walls had to be to hold all of that intense emotion packed tight, so tight no one, not even the man who saved her life, could catch a glimpse of the college girl he'd read about.

How many times did he have to remind himself? Her emotional baggage wasn't his responsibility. His job was to get at the information she had locked in her brain and then get her to safety. That was all.

Change the subject, Norwood. Get out of dangerous territory.

"I have a yoga DVD we can pop in. It'll help you stretch out the soreness."

"Yoga. Mr. CIA-with-a-Gun does yoga."

"Are we going to have this conversation again? I thought we'd already established that your ideas about the CIA are off base."

She shrugged. "I can't seem to help myself. Everything I do is to save lives. It seems your work results in too much loss of life."

"And your way of doing things led you to be tied up on the floor of a deserted shack in the middle of the desert."

She had no quick comeback for that. Ignoring him, she turned back to watch the falling snow, her posture stiff.

"Let's agree to disagree about tactics for the time being, shall we?"

She shrugged at his suggestion. Cal released a slow sigh. Disagreeing would get them nowhere. He scoured his mind for another, lighter topic.

"You know, exercise does help your mental faculties, as well."

"Bill tells me that all the time."

Cal tensed. This was the opening he needed. "You think a lot of Bill Carlisle."

She glanced in his direction. "Yes. Bill's been a good friend...hired me and took me under his wing. He's a great mentor and cares about me. That's why I know I can trust him. Bill would never do anything to hurt me."

"Sometimes the most trusted people make themselves appear that way just to get what they want."

"And you know this because that's exactly what you've been doing for the past two years."

Her snappy remark bit into his conscience. He wished he hadn't brought that particular point to her attention, especially since he'd just vetoed an extraction unit and a way out.

When he didn't respond, she sipped her coffee and turned back to the window. "So you have a car but we can't drive it out of here. A small economy car. For some reason that's not what I expected."

"What did you expect?"

"I don't know. Something small, black and sporty. That's more CIA-style, isn't it?"

He refused to rise to the bait. Drina appeared to like these little mental games of cat and mouse. He suspected she liked them because she usually won. But she wasn't going to win this time. "Small and sporty draws attention. It's my job to fit in."

She looked at him, a rueful smile playing about her lips. "Trust me, Norwood. You'll draw attention no matter what you do."

"Thanks... I think." His grin probably appeared as rueful as hers. Score one for her. The comment also told him she did remember last night or at least recognized the magnetic pull between them. He was glad he wasn't alone on this new, unexplored road. Being attracted to someone he had to protect was a whole new adventure for him. And even then, who would have thought a nerd with black-rimmed glasses would catch his attention?

Always expect the unexpected. That was his motto. He'd certainly forgotten that this time around.

Drina Gallagher was a beautiful young woman. So why did she hide behind those glasses and her work?

Just another mystery Cal would like to solve. Scratch that. Couldn't afford to solve. Drina needed to stay on the other side of *his* wall. He needed to focus on the real mystery…the boss and his gang. He picked what he thought was a neutral topic.

"I suppose you walk everywhere you go."

"No. I drive, but I walk when I have a problem to work on." She turned to face him. "Movement helps me zone out and focus. Sometimes I'll come back to the present and realize I've been walking for hours."

"Well, you built up enough stamina to get you through your kidnapping. We can be thankful for that."

"Yes. Very." Her smile lit up her face. Hazel eyes sparkled. Black bangs swept across her forehead sideways in a flirty way. She was bright, cheerful and beautiful. Just plain beautiful. How did he not see it when they first met? Or maybe this was a new Drina Gallagher…a first appearance of the girl hiding behind the wall.

He forced himself to look at his file in order to stop staring.

"What is that you're studying?"

"Just some notes on my investigation. I thought if I went over them, I might come up with a way to salvage my work."

"Salvage it?" Her lovely face clouded. "See what I mean? We're running for our lives and you keep worrying about catching the bad guys."

Her outburst caught Cal off guard once again. He tried three times to change the subject of their conversation but it just kept coming back to this dangerous arena. Maybe it was time to tackle it.

He took a deep breath to control his biting response and looked at her through a lowered brow. "This from the girl who jumped in front of a raging flash flood to save her computer."

Her hazel eyes sparked and a tinge of red blushed her cheeks. "That…that was different. I… I'm trying to save lives. You're following orders, and those orders usually end up with someone dead."

"My orders are to follow these men and that's an easy job. Wherever Whitson and Carter go, they leave bodies behind. Don't think you are the first one they've put in danger. In fact, you were one of the fortunate ones. An engineer disappeared from the base a little over a year ago. The word put out was that he quit and fled to the Bahamas. The truth is he was snatched off the street. I recognized Whitson's description from an eyewitness."

"You think they killed him?"

"I know they did. He was another of their informants and his information contradicted some I gave them."

"They believed you instead of him?"

Cal nodded. "When I asked about him Carter told me there's lots of abandoned mines in the desert. It was a warning for me not to screw up or I'd end up just like the young engineer."

Her lips parted and she gave a slight shake of her head. "Didn't you feel responsible for his death?"

"Of course I did. But that young man knew he was betraying his country and taking dangerous chances when he got involved with the gang. There were others, innocents who got caught in the crossfire. A sailor they knifed in a guard shack on a San Diego base. A woman and her two children hit by their SUV when they were trying to escape the military police and someone…more personal."

"Who?"

He cleared his throat, not sure he could talk about Buddy. He watched the gentle flakes fall as Buddy's smiling face flashed through his mind.

"Buddy was my best friend. He was like your John. The best of the best. Two agents had infiltrated the gang and were scheduled to meet the boss. Buddy led the team following them for backup. Things went south and Buddy died doing his job…protecting the agents. The boss went underground. I thought the least I could do for Buddy—and the countless others—was bring the boss back to the surface."

She was silent for such a long time, he broke off studying the falling snow and looked at her.

"So it isn't justice you want. You've given up your life to go undercover for revenge. That's the real thing that drives you. You want payback, so you came here instead of going straight back to the base. That's the truth, isn't it?"

He released his breath. "Yes, I admit I want to try and salvage my work. But I headed here because I don't know who to trust on the base and it will take time for my Washington team to get there. I didn't lie to you about that, Drina."

He'd just left out an important detail…like the extraction unit. That thought curbed his argument and something about those hazel eyes, something honest, compelled him to think twice about his next response. "I am a driven person. I'll give you that, but so are you. I don't know many women who'd give up everything to create a weapon to save lives."

He'd hit the nail on the head with that remark. Her lips flattened like she wanted to argue but thought better. Instead, she turned back to the window.

He came to stand beside her. Her brow was creased with a frown. Releasing his breath in another sigh, he caught her shoulders and turned her toward him. Her arms felt slender and fragile beneath his grip. Her features were clouded with doubt and confusion. He wanted to ease her confusion, to make her understand. Shiny locks curled into her face, close to one eye. Unlike the time in the shack, Cal couldn't resist. Reaching up, he smoothed the dark, silky curl away.

"Drina, I think we have the same goal. We don't want to see more people hurt."

She looked up. "And we both feel guilty."

She caught him off guard again with that truth. He inhaled slowly. "Yes, we both feel guilty. And we want to stop the violence."

Closing her eyes she leaned into him. "More than anything."

It was all Cal could do not to wrap his arms around her and pull her close. He bent a little. The warm, soft scent of pine drifted up from her hair. He inhaled deeply, ran his hands up and down her slender arms.

He had a job to do…had to make her understand while there was still time. He could not lose focus again. Gently, he pushed her back.

"I think we might still be able to stop them, Drina. I'm waiting for an email from my handlers. Let's put our wait time to good use, combine our efforts and see if we can't come up with a solid lead. When they contact me, I'll tell them to send in the extraction team."

She opened her eyes, looked up and shook her head. "What can we possibly do?"

He gripped her arms. "I still think you're the key. Somewhere in your mind, something you've seen or heard is the info I need, the clue that will lead me to my next step."

"I've told you everything. I'm not holding anything back."

"I know that, but maybe there's something we haven't touched on, something that seemed unimportant at the time."

Her lips thinned. "The last thing I want to do is to go over the events of the last few days but if you think it will help, I'll do it. Let's start again. From the beginning."

"No. Let's tackle it from a different direction, get a fresh perspective." He dropped his hands from her arms and purposely turned to face the window. He could feel her warm presence next to him, the faint scent of pine. It was too distracting so he walked back toward the couch. Drina followed him and plopped down while he paced in front of the fireplace.

He was silent for a long while. At last he said, "Hal Jacobi."

"Director of Operations at the base?"

He nodded. "What do you think of him?"

"He's okay." She lifted her shoulders in a shrug.

"Just okay? Doesn't sound very positive. Don't you like him?"

"He's a nice guy. Really nice, but he can be a pain to work with sometimes."

"What times? How?"

"He's the kind of person who thinks knowledge is power. He'll say something like, 'My sources tell me your equations don't work,' and all the while his sources are five mathematicians in the back room who could be helping you, talking to you. But he'd rather keep them to himself, you know?"

"You mean he's secretive?"

"Yes, and insecure. He's told me many times these young engineers coming out of school can run circles around him."

"Meaning you."

"Yes, I suppose so."

She paused for a long while and a thought struck Cal. "Did he have access to your computer and emails?"

She nodded slowly. "Yes. Because of the security breach we had a check-and-balance system in place. As head of the program he would have had access to a list of my computer log-ons and offs. He couldn't read my emails but he would have known I logged on, who I contacted and when I logged off."

"So when you fired up your computer to send your equations to Carlisle, he could have seen it?"

Drina perked up. "Yes. Definitely. In fact, it would have sent him an alert since he was program manager here on-site. But he didn't have any direct contact with anything I've done in the last week."

"What about his engineers? Any of them know you cracked the code?"

"Honestly, I was too frustrated to think clearly." She made a wry face and shook her head. "But I don't think so. The test had been a disaster. Everyone involved left early that evening, disappointed and down. I stayed behind to try to figure out what went wrong. The only one who knew anything about my discovery was Bill."

Cal straightened at the mention of her mentor and Drina shook her head. "Don't even go in that direction. I told you, Bill wouldn't do anything to hurt me."

"Carlisle's been at the top of the CIA's investigation list from the beginning, Drina.

Even if you don't think he could be guilty, I have to follow the investigative process, so humor me."

"All right. Ask your questions."

"How did Carlisle sound when you called him."

"Sleepy. I woke him up."

Cal gave her a wry look.

"Sorry, Cal, but he really was sound asleep. I started to talk to him about the numbers and he told me to stop. Not to say another word over his unsecure home phone."

"Then what happened?"

"His warning surprised me. I was so excited I'd forgotten about security so we were both quiet…thinking. And then we heard the clicks, like someone was listening in."

"Carlisle heard them, too?"

"Yes. They worried him. He asked me where my work was. I said on my computer. He told me to follow the protocols, to send it over our secure line and to contact you. And then to get out of there."

"He actually told you to contact me?"

"Yes. Does that sound like someone betraying the program?"

Cal wasn't happy about it, but he agreed. "No, it doesn't. So we're back to square one and Hal Jacobi." He shook his head. "I'll contact my office, see if they can tap into his computer and get some leads. Let's hope we haven't lost internet in this storm."

"Isn't that illegal…or something?"

"His work computer is government property. Everything on it belongs to the US Air Force."

He started toward his bedroom desk.

"Then I can do that."

He paused. "What?"

"I can tap into Jacobi's computer from here. I work extensively with computers. It's part of my job. If Jacobi is hooked into our system, I can access it."

Cal gave a shake of his head. "But can you do it without them tracing it back to your computer?"

"Oh, they'll trace it. But I can set up several proxy servers and lead them around the world. By the time they narrow them down, I'll be gone. They'll know the area but not our exact location. It'll be a tight squeeze and we'll have to time it to the second, but I can do it."

Cal studied her. Her eyes were wide and there was a sparkle in the hazel depths that hadn't been there moments ago. She was excited about the challenge. Brilliant and beautiful. She had all the qualifications to be the perfect CIA analyst. He shook his head at that thought. Maybe in another lifetime. Drina hated the CIA and everything about it...and maybe even him...and he'd allowed himself to be distracted again.

He shook his head and decided to act quickly, before that nagging little voice convinced him otherwise. "Let's do it."

She flashed him a slight smile and spun before her aching muscles reminded her to slow down. Then she winced and gingerly moved forward. He couldn't suppress a chuckle as he followed her to his desk.

She sent him a scathing glance over her shoulder.

"I'm sorry. You really should have taken my suggestion and done a bit of stretching."

Her only response was a miffed silence as she eased into his chair. She pulled her computer out of the backpack Cal had purchased at the sporting goods store and set it on the desk. Cal gave her his internet password and she connected. When it clicked on, he breathed a sigh, relieved they still had a connection.

"It'll take me a few minutes to set things up." Her fingers flew across the keyboard, flitting from site to site. All the while Cal paced behind her. Was he making a mistake?

The smartest thing to do was to let head-quarters do this search. But that would take time and they had precious little of that commodity left. Besides, his team would have to follow protocols and Cal doubted Drina would let the rules slow her down. Time was of the essence. It was a risk, but a risk Cal was willing to take.

"All right. I have the first proxy established. Do you have a watch? I need the response timed to the second."

"Got it."

"Tell me when you're ready."

Cal waited for the second to reach the half hour. "Now."

He heard her fingers tapping the keyboard.

"We're connected. How many seconds?"

"Twenty."

Drina nodded. "All right. I'm going to need at least two minutes' worth."

She searched for another proxy, set up the account and timed the response again. They repeated the process. Tension built in Cal as Drina added seven proxy servers and painstakingly linked them. He couldn't stop pacing or walking to the window and watching the sky outside.

Would they run out of time? Would Drina be able to connect all these sites and still hack into Jacobi's email? Because they'd only get one chance before Drina would have to shut down.

Tension continued to build inside him with no way to release it. He hated this…hated that he was helpless while she did all the work… hated that she was involved at all. He should have called for the team and gotten her to safety.

Maybe his years at his job had skewed his thinking. Maybe she was right. The tactics he'd been using were dangerous, damaging. He certainly felt more comfortable running and firing a gun.

As the minutes ticked by, his concern built. He decided he should have listened to that little voice. "Drina…"

She didn't pause from her furious typing.

"How are you going to get around Jacobi's passwords and safeguards?"

She didn't look up to answer, just kept working with serious determination and a touch of excitement. If he wasn't mistaken, Miss I-Don't-Like-Violence was enjoying this risky venture.

"I won't have to do anything. If our system sent an alert to his email, I'll create a new one and follow the system in." She paused and shot a purposeful grin over her shoulder. "I *own* that program. I'll simply send another alert and follow it past his safety protocols."

"He'll see the alert and know you hacked his account."

"I'll erase it as soon as I'm in."

"We'll be able to read his email?"

"Yes." Now she did pause and turned to face him. "But we'll have limited time. Three maybe four minutes. So tell me now what we're looking for. I won't have time to download everything."

Cal inhaled slowly while his mind churned. "The night you were kidnapped, did he send other emails after he received the alert from my team? That would have been at approximately five in the morning. And if he did, who did he send them to?"

"Got it." She turned back around in her seat. "I'm setting up a search now. The computer can look through his emails much faster than I can. Once we're in, I'll click on the search and download as many emails as I can. But you'll have to time me. I estimate it will take over a minute to connect. A minute to send the alert and track it. And two minutes to copy and download. The proxies will only give us five minutes max. I'll get involved, so give me a countdown to remind me to click off. Everything clear?"

Cal nodded. "I'm still not sure this was a good idea but we're in it now."

"Okay." Drina sat up straighter and took a deep breath. "Tell me when you're ready."

Cal waited for the half minute again. "Go." His tone was low, taut, tense. Drina's fingers leaped over the keyboard. The proxy server appeared and Drina clicked on. The spinning wheel signaling the wait appeared as the link tried to connect. It spun around and around and around.

"Twenty seconds." Still the wheel spun. At last the screen for a new proxy appeared and the wheel spun around as the site hooked up. This time it connected quicker. Another site appeared. Now it seemed the sites were moving faster and faster.

"One minute." Still they hadn't accessed the servers of Drina's company. Cal clenched a fist as he counted the precious seconds clicking by on his watch.

"I'm in."

Cal released the breath he'd been holding and leaned forward to watch the computer screen. Drina clicked through at a speed he couldn't follow.

"Yes!" she yelled but didn't stop typing. "There's the alert. I'm sending another."

She punched a button and the images on the screen froze. One. Two. Three seconds. He was about to ask her what happened when a listing of emails popped onto the screen. Success! Cal wanted to shout this time, but he didn't dare distract Drina.

"Three minutes." He purposely kept his tone low and controlled so as not to alarm Drina, but his heart was pounding. His blood banged so loud through his temples he thought if he leaned any closer to her she'd hear it.

She clicked the search button. An email appeared on the screen.

"There!" Drina's tone reflected her excitement. "Five minutes after five in the morning, he sent an email to someone named Hightower."

Cal bit back an exclamation. Hightower was the engineer with the gambling problem.

More emails popped up on the screen. Drina pointed. "Look. Jacobi sent five…six… no seven emails to Hightower between five and six o'clock after he received the alert. Those two sure were busy the morning I was kidnapped."

Cal straightened with determination. "Get

those emails downloaded. We need to open and read them. They may be the clue I need."

He glanced at his watch. "Four minutes. Hurry."

She hit the keys so fast she started making mistakes. They took precious more seconds to correct.

"Four and a half minutes, Drina. That's enough. Close it down."

"Just a few more. Their emails were shooting back and forth all day long after I disappeared."

"None of that matters if they trace this hack back to us. We can't use the proof if we're dead."

"Just a few more."

"Fifteen seconds, Drina. I said shut it down!"

"Okay. Okay." She punched the exit. The screen went black…but just for a moment. Seconds later, a flashing red box appeared in one corner.

"What's that?" Cal pointed.

"I don't know. I'm not… It's the server. The company's security system is trying to track us."

"Stop it. Shut it down!"

She threw her hands up. "I can't. It used my method and followed our messages back.

It's trying to take over the machine. I can't...
I don't..."

Reaching over Cal punched the off button
on the computer then Drina pulled the plug
on the router. The red light stopped blinking
and the low whir of the computer faded to an
eerie silence.

"We did it!" Exhilaration rushed through
Drina. Cal still leaned over her. With every
nerve in her body tingling, she wrapped her
arms around his neck and hugged him.

Cal froze. With her arms still looped
around his neck, he looked down. Their faces
were inches apart, so close, she could see the
dark stubble of beard on his chin. His gaze
was fixed on her lips and the look in his eyes
made her catch her breath. Gray blue. Intense
and oh-so-serious. Maybe a little angry and
more than a little appealing.

"We did it, Cal. We got your proof." Her
voice was low and soft.

"Did we? Or did we just give away our location?"

Ah. The source of his anger. She understood now. But it didn't change how the look
in his eyes made her feel. Breathless. Needed.
It had been a long, long time since a man
looked at her like that. Too long. Maybe Cal

was right. Maybe it was time she joined the land of the living again. Right now. Right here.

She shook her head only slightly, never taking her gaze off his lips. "No. They didn't trace us. Thanks to your quick thinking, the security software may have pinpointed our area in Southern California but not our exact location."

His mouth thinned. Reaching up, he broke her hands loose from around his neck and shifted his shoulders. "We're not taking any more chances like that."

She took a slow breath. "It didn't feel like a chance. It felt exciting…exhilarating…and we succeeded. So why are you so upset?"

He ran a hand around his neck with an exasperated motion. "What we did is illegal. We just had a discussion about how you hate these kinds of tactics. Now you approve?"

She shrugged. "It was necessary and…" She halted. She'd told Cal multiple times that his tactics were dangerous and violent.

"Okay. Point taken. I see that your work is necessary and sometimes the means are necessary, too. The boss and his men do need to be stopped. But I still think CIA tactics are too violent. And besides…" She couldn't help the grin that stole over her features or her need to touch him.

She leaned in and placed her hands flat on his chest. Taut muscles pushed back against her fingertips, adding to her heightened senses. His lips… That tempting corner she longed to kiss was only inches away. If she just leaned a little closer…

"And besides…" Her tone was an excited whisper. "We just hacked into one of the most sophisticated systems in the country. That was pretty sweet."

SIX

Cal didn't seem to share her enthusiasm. His brow knit in a frown.

"Come on, Cal. Tell me you aren't just a little jazzed that we succeeded. Not to mention the fact that you're really good at this and...like you said, we make a great team."

The frown deepened. "If I were so good, you wouldn't be here right now."

That truth put a cloud over her excitement.

She hesitated. "Well, like it or not, we got at least fifteen emails."

His gazed popped up. "You downloaded that many?"

She nodded.

"Let's take a look at them."

She considered for a moment. For the first time she understood. The thrill, the excitement of what they had done, was still with her. She had never experienced the rush of danger, at least not like this. She was surprised by how much she liked it. Not just the hype of the danger but also the pleasure of the success, of doing something no one else could do. It gave her an inkling of the lure of Cal's work. It was almost like experiencing a new discovery. Doing something no one else had done. But this type of thrill could come with more frequency than a brand-new discovery. It could happen often, weekly, maybe even daily, with every mission. She liked the idea.

Who knew she was an adrenaline junkie? What other things could Cal help her discover about herself?

Her fingertips were still tingling and her stomach was twisted in knots. She… They both needed something to do.

"Could we… Is it safe to take a walk first?"

"Right now?"

She gestured outside. "It's just so…peaceful and beautiful. The storm hasn't hit yet and I…"

She bit her lips, struggling to put into words what she was feeling. "Something like this makes everything so vital. Everything small and great seems remarkable and memorable. I'd just like to stop for a moment and breathe."

He smiled, a wry, twisted lift of his lips. "You never cease to surprise me." He looked around then shrugged. "Why not? A little fresh air might help. Grab your parka."

The air was crisp, cold and silent. Snow had begun to fall again with thick, heavy flakes that made small shushing sounds as they touched the ground.

Cal gestured toward a gully behind his detached garage. Drina led the way down into the culvert. They were surrounded on both sides with white snowy walls and pine trees on the crest above.

They walked in silence, listening to the snow falling. Nothing moved, not even the wind in the pines. They reached a small clearing and Drina turned her face up, letting the flakes fall against her lips.

Peace. She had the strongest sense of peace since her kidnapping. That feeling had a lot to do with the man beside her. His power intrigued her. What he could do stimulated her and at the same time inspired safety and comfort in her. She didn't understand how he could do all those things but she longed for more, felt compelled to get closer. It was time to take a chance. She took a breath. "I wanted to take ballet lessons."

Cal turned toward her, a question forming on his expression.

She rushed to explain. "Yesterday you

asked if I did anything normal when growing up. I wanted to take ballet lessons. It was one of the few 'kid' things I wanted to do."

"And did your parents allow it?"

"Oh, yes. They rarely said no. But my mother never forgot to tell me how I had two left feet, so I dropped it very soon after I started. You know, excellence in all things."

Cal was silent for a long while. Then he turned and began to walk again. "Excellence in all things. Including changing the world. Sounds like a tough way to grow up."

"When your parents are the heads of their respective fields, a lot is expected of you."

"Including not to be a child."

His words caused Drina's defensive hackles to rise. "I suppose you were a Boy Scout and all that."

Cal grinned in a disarming manner. Even if he was making her angry, she couldn't resist that incredible, engaging smile.

"An Eagle Scout, actually. Buddy and I earned our badges doing a project on the president. Our parents even forked out the money for a trip to Washington, DC. We met the president and were fascinated by his security detail. I was hooked and pointed my college classes in that direction when the CIA tapped me for the agency. Buddy followed his father's footsteps into the navy."

"And the rest is history." Sarcasm rode low in her tone.

"Drina, I'm sorry if I hurt your feelings with my comment about your parents. It's just, well, to me that doesn't sound like a fun way to grow up."

"It wasn't. Fascinating. Illuminating. Privileged. But not fun. Never fun. That's why when I got to college, I was determined to find out what 'fun' was all about."

Cal gave a slight shake of his head. "The work you did in college didn't sound like fun. Helping the poor is hard work, not fun."

"Not to me. Looking outside myself, reaching out to others. It was a grand new experience and I loved it. I enjoyed meeting people, leading organizations. It was almost like an addiction. I was caught up in it. I even allowed myself to fall in love."

Cal tilted his head. "You *allowed* it to happen? That's a funny way of putting it. I thought people just fell in love."

"Oh, no. You have to allow it. You have to choose to engage and then to let the emotions go, give them free rein."

"I see. Love doesn't just happen sometimes, in spite of your best intentions?"

She glanced sideways at him, not daring to meet his gaze. Had he stopped talking about her and John? Was Cal trying to discuss their growing attraction? She took a deep breath and her answer was firm. "No. You have to make a conscious decision. There's always a point where you choose to go forward with an appealing relationship or turn away. I most definitely chose to move forward—with devastating consequences."

"Why devastating? Because John enlisted?"

"Yes. At least that's what I thought at the time. My parents implied that my mistakes drove him to it. They said I never should have gotten involved with him in the first place."

"They didn't approve of the relationship."

"No, of course not. They said I was too young. That I had too much to offer the world and shouldn't waste my time in a relationship with a young man with such outdated, illogical ideas."

Cal sighed. "Let me guess. They were referring to John's Christian beliefs."

"Yes."

"Do you believe his ideas were outdated and illogical?"

Her voice dropped. "You mean do I believe in God?" She lifted one shoulder in a slight shrug. "I wanted to. Life with John was so much brighter and better. I wanted the reason for that to be an all-knowing, all-loving God. In spite of all the negativity directed at his faith, John was fun and vibrant and passionate about his love of God. I couldn't bear the thought of my parents ridiculing his ideas, dimming that brightness. That's when I knew they were right. I was far too young."

"I'm not following your logic. You wanted to defend John to your parents, so you broke up with him?"

She stopped and studied the snowy culvert around them. It was hard to put in words what she'd barely even acknowledged in the dark recesses of her mind. "I didn't have the courage to defend him. If I'd truly loved him, I would have stood up for him, championed that shining light in his eyes. Had the strength to believe." She stopped walking and let her head droop.

"But I didn't. I just turned away. Eight months later I found out John had joined the marines and was killed by an unmanned missile attack in Afghanistan."

Cal watched the gentle snow, now falling more steadily. He was silent for a long while. "So your desire to create a weapon to stop those attacks was born out of guilt."

"Yes." She shook her head. "Guilt and vengeance. Like you. Not very good motivations for either of us but especially for you. You have faith. How do you do it?"

"Do what?"

"Justify what you do."

"Are we talking about God now or my work with the CIA again?"

"Both, I guess. I can't imagine giving up my life and pretending to be something I'm not."

He gave a short laugh. "But you're doing the same thing. By your own admission you live like a hermit so you can create a weapon to save lives. I'm not sure how that's so different than what I do. We're both passionate about protecting people. The Lord put that in my heart, and I believe God wants us to do what He puts in our hearts."

She shook her head again. "I wish I had that kind of trust, that kind of faith."

They stood side by side, watching the snow fall gently around them before Cal spoke again. "Faith is a lot like the way you described falling in love. First you have to make a conscious decision, a mental effort. You have to choose God. That opens the door. He takes care of the rest and the heart follows."

"You make it sound easy."

"About as easy as falling in love." He

smiled that winsome, boyish smile that seemed so disarming, so unexpected from the gun-toting agent she knew him to be. It always caught her off guard and warmed her heart. When he smiled like that, he could charm her into believing anything.

"I wish that were true." Her voice was barely above a whisper. "I wish I could fall in love with God as easily as I fell for John or as easily as I could…"

She halted abruptly. Was she about to say as easily as she could fall for Cal? Her gaze jerked up to his. That curious gray blue of his eyes had darkened again. The intensity of his gaze made her heart beat faster.

As Drina felt the blood rushing through her veins it seemed as if something snapped inside her, broke like a dam releasing. Her emotions flooded out. She wrapped her arms around his neck and pulled his head down. His lips were firm and warm against hers. As welcoming and wonderful as she had imagined. They parted.

Then Cal cupped her face with both hands. He tilted her head slightly and kissed her again as if he wanted to make sure what they'd just experienced was real.

The third kiss was just as tender, just as spark filled as the other two. She wanted more, but he broke the kiss and gently moved her away. Cupping both sides of her face, he leaned his forehead against hers. "I think… we'd better stop."

She nodded but didn't really agree. Some barrier had broken inside her. She wanted to feel, to experience more, to allow her senses—long chained by guilt and regret— to break free.

His hands slid down the sides of her neck. She curved her face into him, loving the warmth and comfort of his touch.

Maybe Cal was right. Maybe she wasn't responsible for the world's problems. She was just one woman… One who was falling in love again. That thought jolted her. She couldn't afford to fall in love again. She had work to do. A world-shattering task to accomplish and besides…she might not survive another loss like John's.

Just as that thought occurred to her, Cal squeezed her upper arms and stepped back. Immediately she was cold. Lost. Empty without him.

Too late. It was too late. She was already halfway in love. What would she do now? She wrapped her arms around her waist and held herself together.

Cal ran a hand around his neck. "That won't happen again."

His words hurt even though she'd just had the same thoughts. The hurt must have shown in her face. He grasped her arms again. "You know this is the worst possible time for this to happen."

She shuddered. She couldn't stop herself.

Instantly, he pulled her back into his arms. "Don't misunderstand me. It's wonderful and amazing. But your life is in danger right now. I can't allow my feelings or yours to cloud my judgment, Drina. I have to think clearly…to get you to safety, then we can explore and enjoy what just happened."

She shook her head. "We won't explore this. As soon as this is over, you'll be off to chase the boss and I have to finish my work. Whatever we have will be right here, right now."

He gripped her tighter. "You're right. The boss needs to be stopped but I'll have help. I won't be alone in my mission. You still feel that you have to have excellence in all things. You have to change the world all by yourself. That's not the way it is."

He lifted her chin with his fingertip. "You need to learn that God is in charge. He's the commander and you are just a follower." He ran his thumb over her chin. "You're trying to win the war by yourself. That's too heavy a load for one person to carry."

His hands were warm against skin made cold by the steady breeze. She wanted to capture his hand and hold it close. "What difference does it make? We both want the same thing…are going for the same goal."

"It may seem like I'm splitting hairs, but it's the essence of faith, Drina. I do what I do because I serve Him. I know He's in control. It's not up to me to win the battle against evil. I'm just supposed to find the spy. You want to stop all soldiers from dying." He shook his head. "You want to stop all pain, all hurt, but the world doesn't work like that."

"Maybe that's what's wrong with this world. What kind of all-knowing, all-loving God lets us suffer like this?"

"The kind who wants you to turn to Him, to let Him heal your pain and ease your burdens."

She shook her head, starting to protest, but he placed his fingers on her lips, silencing her. "The world has already been saved, Drina. Jesus did that. He poured out His life for us, for everyone, for all time. He poured Himself into a cup of salvation. All we have to do is accept that cup and follow Him.

"I don't know why John volunteered. But if he was as faithful as you say, I suspect he accepted that cup a long time ago. All he was doing was following in his Lord's footsteps, just as I try to do."

She stared at him. The snow was falling so fast that flakes caught on her lashes. She wiped them away. "You're telling me that I'm not responsible for what happened…for how I abandoned John. I know that now."

He sighed. "There's more. You've said we do what we do out of guilt. I'm saying that there's a difference between shame and guilt. Shame is God's tool. He uses it to make us uncomfortable, to make us examine what we've done. It shows us where we've made missteps, and how to bring those steps to the light and get back on the right path. Guilt is the tool of evil. Guilt makes us hide things. Drives us to make mistakes, pushes us to make choices we would never make if not for the guilt."

The snow had begun to fall thick and hard. The wind slanted at a sharp, painful angle, narrowing visibility. She could barely see the trees above them. She squinted against the gusts.

"But isn't that what you're doing? Letting

survivor's guilt for Buddy make you follow the company's directives without thought?"

He shook his head and had to raise his voice above the whistling wind. "I don't let guilt drive me, Drina. If I did, I'd be with the boss right now and you'd be lying on the floor of the shack with a hole in your head."

She stared at him, silenced by the truth. Then a rustling caught their attention and they both turned to see a large buck leap into the clearing. He turned and froze, long ears twitching. Neither Cal nor Drina moved as the snow fell on the beautiful animal. His stately antlers reaching for the sky, his brown coat sleek. He was majestically poised, and perfect with the flakes falling steadily on his back. The buck's black nose lifted and twitched. Then it seemed his head nodded.

A doe crept out of the bush behind him.

Drina caught her breath. She stood in awe as the two fragile creatures trusted them with their precious, unguarded presence.

Cal slowly reached across the space and linked his fingers through hers. She clung to his hand.

The doe posed, timid and shy, behind the buck, her nose gently lifted in the air as her mate stood guard. After a few moments she made her way across the gully and up the side into the bushes. The buck remained a moment longer, staring directly at them with his oh-so-dark, round eyes. Then with a flick of his tail, he leaped away to follow. Drina released her breath in a wondrous gasp.

The sight made Drina feel special, unique... touched by God. As if He'd chosen this one moment with this one man just for her.

Then another sound echoed outside the clearing. The distant whine of an engine sent ripples of fear shooting up Drina's spine.

"Is that a quad?"

"A snowmobile. We have to get back."

Cal turned and pulled Drina behind him, back the way they'd come. The storm's cold breath bit into them. Cal dragged her, slipping and sliding over the snow as they tried to outrun the ever-increasing rage of the blizzard and the drone of the snowmobile. His lungs seared with each breath and his thighs burned from struggling through the drifts. How much more was Drina suffering?

Why had he let them move so far away from the cabin?

Drina said something about burning but he couldn't hear clearly over the shrieking wind. He raised his gaze and saw the cabin ahead of them. He pulled her onto the front porch with the wind snarling behind them, opened the door and almost pushed her inside.

"Go to the bedroom, where the blinds are closed."

She followed his directions and moved toward the bedroom, tracking mud all the way.

"Plug in the router. See if we have a connection."

Drina dashed to the desk, pulling her gloves off as she went. Cal stalked across to the wall safe. He pulled off his gloves, dripping melting snow on the credenza beneath him. With fingers stiff from cold, he punched the code into the safe and pulled out his gun. He jammed a cartridge in and checked the bullet in the chamber.

The clicks of her fingers sounded on the keyboard behind him as he stalked back to the door and peeked into the living room.

He held his breath as the noise of the snowmobile engine came closer, pausing just outside the front door of the cabin. One…two…three seconds. The engine revved.

Cal caught a glimpse of the man's face before he ducked back behind the edge of the door. The gun clicked as he released the safety. He was pretty sure he knew the guy from town. He released his breath slowly but didn't move until he heard the sound of footsteps pounding on the wood porch.

"Hello? Anybody there?" The words were muted by the whistling wind. It seemed like forever before footsteps stalked back across the porch and the engine revved as the snowmobile sped off.

Cal clicked the safety back into place on his gun and leaned his head against the wall.

That was too close. He'd slipped up again. Drina made him lose all sense of caution.

"Is he gone? Have they found us?" Drina's harsh whisper echoed across the room.

"I'm not sure, but I think I recognized him. I believe he's with the volunteer fire department here. Probably on a run to check the outlying cabins before the storm gets worse."

He could hear her sigh of relief from where he stood. The sound pierced him like a needle. She was relying on him to keep her safe. So far, he'd been doing a lousy job.

He looked back over his shoulder and kept his voice low. "Were you able to connect?"

"No. No reception. I had it for a moment before that last blast of wind."

"Just as I expected. The storm's too powerful even for my satellite." The community was cut off and hunkering down for a serious storm, as was evidenced by the volunteer firefighter checking the cabins. The fireman also left in a hurry, probably trying to make it back to safety before the storm unleashed its full fury…which sounded like it just happened. Cal's cabin rattled like an earthquake had hit.

Drina let loose a little squeak. Cal caught himself. Gritting his teeth, he purposely released a long, slow breath and stepped away from the wall. They needed to dial down the stress, and that wouldn't happen as long as they were trapped in this room.

"Stay here. I'm going to take a look."

He peeked around the corner. Staying close to the wall, he edged to the large window and looked out as far as he could see… which wasn't far. The snow was coming down hard and fast, slanted at an angle by the sharp wind. He could only see a few feet beyond the cabin.

No sign of the snowmobile or the rider. In fact, snow had already obliterated his tracks. Cal moved to the kitchen to examine that side of the house. No sign of movement or activity. Then to Drina's room and finally, he returned to his own room and raised a blind.

"It's clear on all sides."

Drina slid her hood back and unzipped her parka with trembling fingers.

"Are you cold?"

She nodded.

"Sorry. A fire would be nice, but I don't think it's wise to light one just yet. Let's find you some dry clothes and I'll fix you something warm to drink."

He placed his gun in the safe but didn't seal it shut. He wanted it accessible if he needed it quick. Then they walked to the living room, where he took off his coat and gestured for Drina to sit. She handed him her damp parka then plopped on the couch and wrapped the throw around her. Cal hung the parka near the back door to dry.

In minutes he returned to the front room and placed a cup of steaming hot chocolate in Drina's hands. She gripped both palms around the heat and blew on it before taking a sip. When she finished, a blot of whipped cream clung to her upper lip. He handed her a napkin. She took it with fingers that still trembled.

Wiping whipped cream off her lips, she said, "Now what do we do?"

He sighed as a weight settled down on him. "We wait. The storm may have us locked in but that means the boss and his team are locked out. I'm hoping once my handlers realize they've lost contact with us, they'll send out an extraction team."

Her posture perked up. "Is that standard procedure?"

Cal hated to dash her hopes but lying would be worse. "No. But nothing about this case is standard procedure, especially since you've arrived on the scene. I figure they'll have a team in the air soon, if they don't already."

"So they could be here in a few hours."

Cal shook his head. "They'll be just as hampered by the storm as we are, Drina. They'll be in the area, as close as they can get. But they'll have to wait out the storm, too."

"Oh." She sagged deeper into his brown leather couch. "So what do *we* do now?"

"Are you hungry?"

"Starved."

"You should be. We missed breakfast and lunch." He moved to the kitchen and opened the refrigerator. "Let's see what we can rustle up. Do you like strawberries?"

"Yes."

"Perfect." He pulled the bag of frozen items out of his freezer and got to work. Soon the smell of bacon drew her toward the peninsula separating the small kitchen from the large family/living room. Leaning her elbows over the counter, she surveyed the foods scattered across it.

"What are you making?"

"Crepes filled with cheese and smothered in strawberries." He deftly flipped a very thin, slightly browned crepe in the pan.

"It's a good thing we won't be here for long. I could get used to this and I think my trim figure would suffer."

"Well, you don't stay trim by working out so I have to assume you don't cook, either."

She laughed. "Cup-a-Soup and Chinese takeout with plenty of fresh fruit are my gourmet foods of choice. Grab and Go is my motto."

"Then I'll have to do my best to improve your health and broaden your tastes."

"Improve my health…with bacon?"

He smiled. Quick-witted and capable. He loved how she kept him on his toes. "Frankly, I don't have much time to cook, either, so when I'm here, I indulge."

"Please, don't let me stop you. Indulge away."

He grinned. "My pleasure."

She looked around. "I thought for sure you'd sing while you cook."

"Trust me, it's better I don't sing. That's why I stayed in the kitchen with my mom."

"Too bad. I could have used a little music right now."

"I thought you didn't care for it."

"I didn't say I didn't like it. I said we didn't have much of it around…except Beethoven and Bach, of course. My dad was a big believer in classical music stimulating a child's mental capacity, so I always had it playing in my room while I worked."

Drina shook her head. "When I got to college, I realized how much I was missing, so I took a music appreciation class."

Something caught her eye and she wandered toward the cabinet. The whole bottom was filled with LPs.

"Wow. You are quite a collector." She pulled one of the snugly packed LPs loose. "Who is this?"

"The quintessential female jazz singer of the thirties. She had a very rough life but her voice and phrasing…" He gave a shake of his head. "Reaches right down into your soul and takes a hold of it."

She ducked her head. "I'd like to listen to her sometime. I'd like to—" she shifted her shoulders "—experience my soul."

Cal paused to study her.

She answered his look with another awkward shrug. "I've been so locked in, so closed up for such a long time, I'm not sure I have a soul." She laughed. "I don't even know what one feels like."

He strode across the kitchen and grasped her hand where it rested on the counter. "Trust me, Drina Gallagher, you have a soul. A beautiful one. Any woman who has devoted her entire being to saving lives has to have one."

She looked up and the sincerity in her hazel eyes pierced his heart. "Are you sure, Cal? Because if I had a soul, don't you think I'd know God, see Him in my life?"

He lifted her hand to his lips and kissed the soft, pale skin between the knuckles. "I'm sure. And God has always been in your life. You just haven't recognized Him."

She squeezed his palm. "Where, Cal? Where is He? In your jazz singer's sad songs?"

He nodded. "There. But not just in sadness. He's in good food and good friends. Conversations... Even intellectual ones that solve the world's problems." He kissed her hand again. "He's even in a little girl's joy when she spins across the floor in ballet moves."

She smiled, shy and sweet. "So I missed out in more than one way."

"It's not too late for lessons. Never too late."

The smile faded. She disengaged her hand and shook her head. "Two left feet, remember?"

Just like that the hopeful moment was gone. Drina's walls went back up and Cal realized why they were so strong. She'd built them with a lifetime of insecurities…the kind only God could heal.

With a sigh, he turned back to his food preparations. While he worked, he tried to lighten the mood. He talked about music again, the Jazz Age, the folk movement, soft rock and eighties electronic music and how it impacted his teen years. Finally, placing both hands on the counter, he leaned low enough to see beneath the cabinet. "Just think, we've barely scratched the surface of the great musicians, and movies…well, let's not even go there."

"I'm not a big fan of movies."

"Really? Why not?"

She leaned against the breakfast bar so close, Cal could smell her soft pine scent. "Where should I begin? They're full of clichés, trite plots and sappy endings. The heroes and heroines are so unrealistic. I mean come on…a treasure-hunting female who lives in a multimillion-dollar house and can fight off six bad guys with her bare hands. How silly can you get?"

"I don't know. I saw a female with no experience fight off one bad guy. She made him dive off the side of a hill."

His statement made her laugh. "That was pure adrenaline."

He bent low again to emphasize his words. "That was pure bravery."

Drina paused. "You think I'm brave?"

"I know you are. Not many men would have left the cover of the rocks or had the sense to get in my car and drive it straight at Carter."

She couldn't seem to face his honest admiration. She looked down.

"You're pretty good yourself, rushing in to rescue me and driving us through the desert. I still don't know how you wrangled that ATV through the riverbed. You have to have muscles of steel."

His shook his head. "I'm not a superman, Drina." The image of the murdered engineer flashed through his mind, quickly followed by Buddy's smiling face and all the others. He was letting them all down, including Drina. She wasn't safe yet and no one else in the boss's path would ever be safe again.

Unaware of his dark thoughts Drina said,

"I don't know. A guy who can shoot like a cowboy and cook like a chef is pretty super in my eyes."

He smiled slightly. Her attempt to salve his wounded ego helped a little. He plopped the plate down in front of her. "Taste this and we'll continue your education on fine dining."

Strawberries spooned over golden crepes stuffed with cream cheese filling. Drina picked up her fork and almost dived in before Cal dipped his head and clasped his fingers together. She halted, fork midair as Cal began.

"Lord, we thank You for saving us and for the storm that's keeping us safe. We also thank You for the chance to listen and laugh and remember."

As soon as he said *amen*, Drina cut off her first piece of crepe. Another bite went into her mouth, and another before Cal could even walk around and sit beside her.

"This is…" Speaking with her mouth half-full, she stopped, covered her mouth with her hand and finished chewing before she spoke again. "This is probably the best crepe I've ever eaten…bar none. The best."

She paused, staring at him, then popped another bite into her mouth, not bothering to finish chewing this time. "Is there anything you don't know?"

He frowned. "Yeah, I can't figure out the identity of one very important man."

SEVEN

Cal's somber tone brought the shadows back into the room. Drina placed her fork on her plate. "You would know by now…if I hadn't interfered."

Cal shrugged. "You know, I've been giving that a lot of thought. I'm not sure that's true. It's likely you didn't interfere. If anything, you just provided them the opportunity they needed to test me."

"I don't understand."

"Think about it. You'd barely scratched the surface on your discovery. It's going to take more work to bring it to a functioning level. Who's better qualified than you to do that?"

Shrugging her shoulders, she shook her head. "No one."

"Then why were they so anxious to kill you before your work was done?"

"I guess they thought they could do it without me."

Cal's lips thinned into a straight, determined line. "No. They needed you. What they didn't need was a questionable informant like me. They needed to prove my unquestionable loyalty."

"Wait…are you saying they set up my kidnapping just to test you?"

"No. Something forced their hand."

"What?"

He shrugged. "The clicks on Carlisle's phone. I think they were CIA wiretaps. He realized we were close so he panicked and told Whitson and Carter to snatch you and make a run for it."

She tensed and gave him a hard look. "Or maybe Jacobi's men were tapping Bill's line. Since he got the alert from our server, maybe he decided to have his men kidnap me before I could get the info to Bill."

"It's possible."

Drina was glad he conceded her point. Nothing Cal could say would sway Drina's confidence in her mentor. "I trust Bill implicitly."

"Like you trusted your parents?"

"What's that supposed to mean?"

He shifted his shoulders uncomfortably, obviously aware that he'd treaded on dangerous ground. "You ended a relationship because your parents didn't like the guy and you've felt guilty ever since. Don't you think it's time you made your own decisions, based on your own feelings?"

Anger flashed through Drina. "Feelings? It's always about feelings with you. What about facts? Evidence. Four years of working day to day with Bill tells me I know him."

He shook his head. "Drina, you're not sure about your own reasons and motives. How can you possibly be so sure about someone else's?"

She didn't have an answer for that. And the truth of it stung. Deeply. She'd spent a great deal of time telling him how little she trusted herself. Now she regretted it. Regretting being open and honest with him at all.

In the sudden silence, they heard sleet beating against the windows like pellets. The ping of the snow was almost painful. A constant reminder of the zinging bullets they'd been avoiding for days.

She studied him, her brow furrowed. It was time to get back to safe ground...ground she understood...the kind that would help. She clenched her fingers. "We still have the emails. Let's read them and find out what Jacobi was up to after he had me kidnapped."

Cal gave her a steel-eyed blue glare before

he nodded. "Good idea." He carried the plates to the sink while Drina retrieved her computer from the bedroom and plopped down on the couch. He sat down next to her and she scooted away, putting more space between them. Thankfully, before he could comment, the emails popped up.

She pointed to the computer. "This is the alert and this is Jacobi's first email to Hightower."

Cal nodded. "He's one of Jacobi's engineers. We've been watching him, as well."

Drina read the email out loud. "'This is a follow-up to the pyramid alert just sent to your phone. There's trouble at the lab.'" She paused. "What's a pyramid alert?"

"Standard emergency procedure. Once I arrived at the test site and found your abandoned car, I contacted my team. Since Jacobi is the lead project manager they contacted him to institute a telephone alert system about a possible security breach. Jacobi calls the next man down from him and that man calls the next down the list until everyone has been verbally contacted by phone."

"But Jacobi is doing more than verbally contacting Hightower. He's sending private emails."

Cal pointed to the long list of emails. "I

imagine after Jacobi got the call and started the pyramid alert, he probably checked his own emails. That's when he would have seen the alert from your company's system. Obviously he was pretty riled and started sending texts to Hightower. Maybe you were right. Maybe the leak is Jacobi and Hightower is in on it. Let's see what they talk about."

Drina opened the first reply. "Hightower says, 'What kind of trouble?' Jacobi replies, 'Drina Gallagher is missing.' Then Hightower says, 'After the test today I don't blame her for taking off. That was a disaster.'" Drina made a sound. "A disaster that turned into a breakthrough."

Cal ignored her comment and started to read out loud. "'She didn't leave on her own. It looks like she attempted to send something through email, but it didn't go…or she cancelled it. Then she disappeared. There's signs of a struggle near her car.'"

Cal slowed as he continued to read. "'You think she was trying to contact Carlisle in a way that couldn't be traced?'

"'We'll never know. We have no record of what she wanted to tell him or even if she was successful.'

"'Sounds like your suspicions were correct.'"

Suddenly, the computer screen went black.

Cal caught his breath. "What happened? What's wrong?"

"Power. The battery's dead."

He studied Drina. "Did you do that on purpose? They were close to giving us an answer."

She threw her hands up. "I can't make it run if it doesn't have power."

"You don't have a charger?"

"Of course I do. It's in the backpack you threw down the muddy river."

His brow furrowed. "Oh, of course." He thought for a moment then popped up from the couch. "Let me see if I've got one that'll work."

Drina followed him. But nothing he had matched. Silently, Drina sagged. They returned to the living room. Cal dropped to the couch. Drina sat, too, and placed the computer on the cushion between them, then stared out the window, never meeting Cal's gaze.

He rose. "Are you still cold?"

She nodded and pulled the throw tighter around her. She couldn't tell if she was trembling from cold or fear or maybe even anger.

"I'll start a fire."

"I thought you said it wasn't safe."

"That firefighter is long gone and the

storm is raging. I doubt anyone will smell the smoke."

He stacked twigs and small logs in the fireplace and lit them. After a long while he said, "Drina…"

"Don't, Cal. Don't say it. I don't believe it. Not for a minute. Jacobi is trying to throw suspicion off himself by accusing Bill."

"Why would he do that?"

"Why would Bill tap his own phone?"

"I told you. It might have been a CIA wiretap. I was waiting for my handlers to confirm that before we lost contact."

She stared at him. It hurt too much to think of Bill as a traitor, to think that she'd misjudged a person or the situation so badly. She couldn't do it. She gave a shake of her head. "I don't believe it. Bill wouldn't hurt me."

She sat in the corner of the couch, pulled up her legs and wrapped her arms around them. She felt so fragile, so close to breaking.

Cal took a deep breath. "You're not alone, Drina. No one ever really knows what drives people. Most of us don't understand why we do what we do let alone—"

She cut him off. "It's not Bill. It can't be. I know him. He wouldn't… If I can't trust him, who can I trust?"

That was the real question. The deep, shadowed one she'd refused to face. Who was right? John and Cal with their hopeful faith or her parents with their logic and facts? She needed answers. Facts. Proof of Bill's betrayal...of God's existence. Not wispy promises.

Cal's voice was low when he spoke. "I think you know the answer to that, Drina. People fail. Let us down. But God never does. If you're losing hope and faith, maybe it's because you're putting your faith in the wrong place."

She turned to Cal with an angry retort. But before she could speak, the lights popped off. Instead of yelling at him, she cried out and reached for him. He grasped her hands and pulled her close.

"It's all right." His voice was calm and sure. His arms a safe haven from the storm inside Drina as well as out. She buried her face in his neck, thankful for that simple comfort.

"The storm knocked out the electricity, that's all. It happens a lot up here. Frankly, I'm surprised we had power for as long as we did."

She bobbed her head in a nod, not sure he felt it as she clung to him.

"I have a backup generator in the garage for just these kinds of situations. I can go out and start it, if you like."

Her eyes had grown accustomed to the dark. The orange glow of the fire gave his oh-so-perfect face a golden sheen. His features were creased with concern…for her. It was difficult to stay frustrated with him when he was trying so hard to take care of her.

She nodded her chin toward the white snow slashing across the picture window. "That means you have to go out into that." She shook her head. "I don't think so."

Cal gripped her hand. "All right, then."

He knew she wanted to say more but the angry words floated away as they sat in the dark; the fire crackled as the storm howled and shook the house.

He tried to keep his voice low, controlled. "We're going to sleep in here, closer to the fire. It'll be warmer in here since we don't have a furnace. I'll even give you the couch."

Releasing her hand, he fluffed the pillows and pushed her into the corner. Drina snuggled in, tucking her chin under the covers as he spread knitted throws around her. Then he sat on the floor in front.

She sighed and snuggled a little deeper into the pillows. After a long while, she suddenly pushed up again. "Is your real name even Cal Norwood?"

Her hazel eyes reflected the sparks of the fire. A stubborn curl had fallen over her forehead. He pushed it back, slowly, loving its silky feel against his fingertips.

"Yes, that's my real name. The agency didn't change my identity. They just invented the gambling addiction that supposedly estranged me from my family and friends and sent me right into the arms of desperation. And believe me, I acted the part. I'm not proud of some of the things I had to do."

He brushed the curl again, sweeping it slowly to the side, letting his fingertips linger on her skin. "I've been playing deceitful Cal for so long, I almost forgot the real me. The guy who loves music, good food and beautiful women."

"Do I count as a beautiful woman?"

He chuckled. "Yes. You are beautiful in your own understated way. I don't know how I... How any man could miss it. But it probably has something to do with how very brilliant and serious you are, especially when you hide behind glasses bigger than your whole face."

Then he tucked the covers under her chin again.

Drina closed her eyes. Her voice was just

above a murmur. "Cal, I think we saved each other."

He watched Drina fall asleep, wishing they could have more moments like this, that he could keep her safe forever. He rested his hands on the edge of the couch and his chin on top of them. He could almost see the two of them here, in his living room, the fire crackling, a big golden retriever at her feet. His eyes drifted shut.

Did she like dogs?

Alarm bells clanged somewhere in this image of Drina ruffling the fluffy golden fur of the dog's head. The animal barked.

Barked?

Cal jerked awake. No dog. No barking. There was no sound at all. Not the howl of wind from the storm outside. Not even the crackle of the fire.

The fire was out. The room was dark…except for the red laser beams crisscrossing the air above him.

He rolled onto all fours and shook Drina. "Wake up. They've found us. We have to get out of here."

She made a choked sound and tried to rise but he pushed her back down. "Shhh… Stay low. Roll off the couch and crawl toward the back door. I'll meet you there."

"Where are you going?"

"After my gun and your computer. I'm not taking a chance on you running back for it again."

EIGHT

Adrenaline surged through Drina. She did as Cal instructed, rolling to the floor. On all fours, she scurried to the kitchen and the small niche where his washer and dryer faced a solid wood door. On hooks nearby, she saw their heavy parkas where Cal had hung them earlier. Her shoes sat on the floor below.

She slipped them on and tied them tightly. As she slid her arms through the sleeves of her jacket, the door handle above her turned… once…twice. Holding her breath, she scooted into the corner, expecting bullets to pierce the wooden portal any moment. Nothing happened.

Crouching low, Cal came around the corner, gun in hand.

She grasped his arm. "There's someone out there," she whispered.

"I'm sure they have a guard at each door." His voice was raspy and slightly out of breath.

He handed her the backpack. "Zip up and put this on."

She looked down as her zipper snagged. "If they have someone at every door, how are we going to get out?" She got it loose and pulled up just in time to see Cal's grim features.

"I'm going to distract them."

"How?"

"Don't think about that. Just follow my instructions. When I say go, run to the back of the garage."

"The back? Aren't we going to the car?"

"My little car won't make it on these roads. Those men didn't drive up into my driveway. I would have heard their engines. You remember their big loud SUVs? They had to leave them on the main road."

She nodded.

"The road is just beyond where we walked this morning. The little culvert where we saw the buck and doe? If you keep going maybe forty or fifty feet straight, you'll see the road. Follow it until you find their cars."

"Follow it? Aren't you coming with me?" Her tone had risen above a whisper and he motioned her volume down with his hand.

"I'm coming, but I'm going to try to delay them. If we get separated, I don't want to arrive at the car and have to double back for you."

He leaned in close. "Keep your head down. Run as hard as you can and don't look back. Got it?"

"Yes, but…"

"No questions, Drina. Just do as I say."

She sealed her lips and nodded.

Cal edged to the corner and looked around the wall to the front door. Pulling something small and round out of his coat pocket, he pressed a button and rose slowly to his feet.

A red light flashed down the kitchen straight to the back wall of the laundry niche. Cal jerked back behind the corner, out of the beam's way. But as soon as it disappeared, he stepped into the center of the opening and pulled back his arm, preparing to throw the small round object in his hand.

Just as he did, the electricity came on and the lights in the house flared to life, leaving Cal completely exposed. Several beams flashed down the hall.

Drina screamed and Cal's arm shot forward. Gunshots shattered the big picture window just as Cal ducked around the corner. Drina heard the ping of something metal as the object Cal had thrown struck the front door and exploded.

Drina covered her ears and ducked. The whole house rocked and shook. Glasses and plates in the kitchen fell from the cabinets and shattered. The coffee machine flew past them, bouncing on the floor and landing against the back wall.

Drina stared at it in horror. But Cal was already on the move. He threw the lock on the door, shoved it open and peeked out. Frozen in shock, Drina watched him take aim and fire. The gunshot made a soft, funny sound. Then Cal grabbed her arm, pulling her to her feet.

"Go now. Run, Drina!"

With no time to think, she dashed across the pristine snow. The pure white landscape was so bright, she had no trouble seeing. Another explosion rocked the house and she looked over her shoulder to see the kitchen wall explode outward.

Thoughts flashed through her mind. Cal had a silencer and more ammunition hidden somewhere in his safe house.

A gas line had been hit. Or maybe sparked by broken electric lines.

Cal's home was exploding. *His record collection.*

Drina's breath came out in a sob. Just as

she reached the garage, a motion detector light kicked on.

Electricity. The light would draw the men's attention. She heard another sound behind her. Several muffled shots. Ignoring Cal's warning, she glanced over her shoulder. Cal fired shots toward the front of the house.

She reached safety behind the garage, bent over to catch her breath and turned to look back. She saw a blur out of the corner of her eye, and Cal pushed her roughly forward.

"Run! Don't stop till you reach the cars."

Spurred on, Drina dashed away, this time not daring to pause for breath or look back. The cabin rested on a slight rise and she ran down the incline into the culvert, almost tripping. The snow slowed her down. At least a foot high, it was even deeper in the ravine. With each step, she had to lift her feet high to free them from the sucking, frozen white powder.

She trudged on but didn't hear Cal following. Only more gunfire, muzzled and now followed by rapid shots from an automatic weapon. The men had found Cal and were firing back.

Drina's breath came out in another sob. The freezing air burned her lungs and the sob ended in a cough. In the empty, white, death-like silence, every small sound echoed in the little ravine. Suddenly aware that her noises were carrying, especially above her, she looked up, tripped and fell face-first in the thigh-deep snow.

Ice filled her nose and mouth. Smothering, she struggled to turn over in the deep drift. Lying flat on her back, she gasped for air. Sharp, icy pain seared through her chest. Hot tears flowed down her frozen cheeks. She faced a dark, midnight sky, full of frosty diamond stars.

Where was Cal? Why wasn't he following her?

More shots pierced the air. Cal's words came back to her. *Run and don't look back. I don't want to have to double back for you.*

What if he took another route to the road? Maybe he was already headed for the car with those men close behind. Waiting for her could put him in more danger.

That thought spurred her to move. Rolling to her side, she pushed up from the drift, stumbled to her feet and slugged forward.

Nothing looked familiar. She didn't remember going this far on their walk. Had she missed something? Was she walking farther away, lost in the woods?

Beyond the white walls of the culvert, everything seemed swallowed in darkness. In fact, everything was silent. She no longer heard shots from the cabin. Was Cal hurt, wounded and bleeding? *Was he dead?*

Drina ran, panting and kicking the snow as she staggered forward. Up ahead, the culvert curved. Bushes hung over the edge. Flattened by the weight of the snow, they looked different, but they were definitely where the buck and doe had hidden.

Her thighs burning, Drina climbed out of the culvert. At the top, she paused and looked around. Cal said forty or fifty feet more. How could she measure forty or fifty feet in this vast white sameness?

Straight forward. Just go straight forward.

She picked a tree about the right distance away. It had a distinctive knoll she couldn't mistake or lose and she lunged straight for it, finding speed now that the deeper drifts didn't slow her. The total silence behind spurred her on.

Please, Lord. Please let me find the car and let Cal be waiting for me.

Suddenly, she stumbled into a clearing and halted. Looking down, she saw a wide strip with black asphalt below tire tracks. The clearing was the road!

Her gaze jerked back and forth along the

road. To her left, three black SUVs were parked in the middle of the road. A man stood near the front of the lead car. Drina's heart leaped. Cal!

The man stepped away and hurried toward her. She started to run also, but her eyelashes were full of frost and her eyes stung. Her vision blurred with pooled tears.

Something wasn't right. She wiped a hand furiously across her face, then stopped abruptly, sliding on the iced-over asphalt.

The man wasn't Cal.

He raised the gun in his hand, taking careful aim. Drina caught her breath.

From the trees beside the guard, a dark blur dived at him. The man didn't have time to fire or even turn. Cal was on him before he could change direction. They fell to the ground and slid across the road. The man's gun flew from his grasp and into the ditch.

Cal landed on top. Still holding his gun, he struggled to get to his feet but his footing slipped out from beneath him and he fell heavily to the side.

The man pushed upward, rising above Cal, but his feet slid, too. Powerless to stop his forward momentum, the guard fell forward, arms outstretched to stop his fall. As he came down, Cal rolled toward him, swung and struck the man's chin with the butt of his gun. The guard fell flat and didn't move.

Cal rose, carefully placing his feet. Drina ran forward and almost bowled him over as she threw her arms around him.

Prying her loose, he pulled her toward the car. "We have to hurry."

As they reached the closest vehicle, he opened the door, grabbed the keys out of the ignition and tossed them into the dark woods. He did the same with the next. When they reached the last car, he pushed her toward the passenger side. Drina had just opened the door when another explosion rocked the forest. Flames jumped above the treetops.

"Oh, Cal. Your home."

She looked at him through the open doors. His features settled into something hard and grim. "Get in."

He slid in without another word. With one last glance back, Drina climbed inside. Cal put the vehicle in gear and eased the car around, careful to avoid the ditches on both sides.

Drina held her breath as the big vehicle slipped on the ice and slid precariously close to the edge. Cal eased to a stop and shifted to four-wheel drive. As the gears kicked in, he pressed on the accelerator. To Drina's relief, the wheels caught and moved down the road, crunching icy snow beneath them.

Drina released a breath she didn't know she'd been holding. She closed her eyes and leaned back. Something on the dash began to beep and she jerked up to see the seat belt symbol.

"Buckle up." Cal didn't take his gaze off the road.

The incongruity struck Drina and she laughed, giving in to sudden, overwhelming relief, but Cal's harsh features never eased. Her own smile faded in the face of his bleak expression.

Wet and cold, she shivered and reached for the heater controls. She had to search for them on a dash full of electronic equipment. She didn't recognize any of the symbols. At last she found one she thought was the heater and gave it a tentative punch. Hot air flowed out of the vents and Drina raised her hands, turning them over in the warmth.

"Take your coat off so your clothes have a chance to dry."

Thankful for something to do, she pulled the backpack off her shoulders and unzipped. By the time she'd thrown them both in the back seat, her fingers were beginning to tingle with the heat.

As Cal turned onto a main road, Drina rubbed at her prickling cheeks and hands. Cal's white-knuckle grip on the steering wheel made her nervous. Maybe she needed to keep her coat and computer closer.

"Where are we going?"

"Back to the base as fast as we can go."

"I thought you said it wasn't safe."

"My house is...*was* a safe house. Most safe houses have a beacon that sends a signal to headquarters. Now that it's been destroyed, the beacon will cease. My handlers will immediately send extraction teams to preapproved meeting points. At this time the safest one is on the base."

Drina studied his face in the shadows. She saw nothing familiar in the harsh features that hours ago had seemed so dear.

"Does that mean... Cal, did you set off the second explosion? Did you destroy your own house?"

"Yes." His lips sealed into a hard, thin line.

"I'm so sorry..."

"Don't feel bad for me. I deserved to lose my home."

She caught her breath. "I... I don't understand."

They reached the main road. This larger thoroughfare had already been plowed. He turned onto the smooth, wide street and sped up but he didn't release his grip on the wheel.

"The simple truth is you could—should—have been on your way to another safe location. My house would have been empty when they arrived. But I asked my handler to hold off, so I could find a way to salvage my work."

It took a long moment before his words sank in. She shook her head. "It's not your fault. You didn't know. You thought your house was safe." She paused. "How *did* they find us?"

"Because I wasn't doing my job. They planted another tracker on you. Once I found the first, I should have checked, should have thought to look for more. But I was too busy feeling sorry for myself, and afterward I was too…distracted. Now we're on the run again. I'm the one who should be apologizing."

"Distracted. You mean by me?" Cal didn't answer.

Whatever Drina meant to say next was silenced by a crackling radio on the dash. She jumped as the disembodied voice flowed through the car. "Philips? Do you copy?"

Cal turned up the volume and leaned in closer.

"Yeah. I'm here."

"They got away. Stole Carter's car."

Cal leaned back, a smile flitting over his lips. Obviously, he derived some satisfaction in the fact that he'd chosen the car that belonged to Carter.

"We think they're headed down the mountain. Set up a blockade at the highway. Stop them before they reach the main freeway."

Another voice crackled. Drina recognized Carter's. "Can the chatter, you idiots. Norwood's got his own radio."

The radio clicked loudly and the static ended in silence. Cal turned the dial off.

"Well, I guess that answers that. They must have had spare keys. Both vehicles are up and running. Now the two of them are close behind us."

They came to the two-lane main street. Streetlights cast a yellow tint on the pristine snow, and muddy slush already filled the gutters. Instead of slowing, Cal sped up, though the speed limit was lower.

"Aren't you worried about attracting attention?"

Cal shook his head. "At this point I'd be happy to see a policeman, but I'm sure they're all assisting the outlying residents."

They came to an intersection and he made a quick turn. The back end of the car slid across the road. Drina cried out and Cal eased off the gas.

"Sorry. It came up on me suddenly."

"What do you mean *it*? Is there another route down off the mountain?"

Cal didn't answer. This dark, intense Cal was a stranger.

He slowed, turned right and came to a full stop. A large yellow caution sign blocked the middle of the road. The words in bold, black letters read Closed. Do Not Pass.

Drina glanced at Cal as he accelerated and drove around the sign. The road had been plowed even though it was closed to traffic. A narrow ribbon of black, just wide enough for one car, stretched down into inky blackness.

Drina looked at Cal again. His shoulders tensed. He might not be willing to look at her but he seemed acutely aware of her every move...every concerned look she sent his way.

He tilted his head to the side, almost as if he was trying to ease a pain in his neck. "I think they sent plows from Bakersfield to help. They probably took this route since it's shorter, but the road is steep and twisting. It's too dangerous for the public. That's why it's blocked off. It follows the path of the Kern

River down the mountain. It won't be easy-going, but we don't have a choice."

Drina focused on the narrow ribbon of black road. Some of Cal's grim attitude seeped into her. He was picking and choosing which of her questions he would answer. Was that because he didn't want to tell her about the danger they were heading into?

If true, how many other things had he purposely not mentioned? As they sped down the steeply inclined, slick highway, Drina had to admit her confidence in Cal had been severely shaken.

They drove for a long, tense while before Cal bit off a soft, muttered sound.

"What? What's wrong?" She glanced up to see his gaze fixed on the rearview mirror.

Before she could turn around to look, he said, "Drina, are you wearing the shoes I bought you?"

"Yes. My other shoes are…were in your cabin."

"So the only thing that is yours originally is your computer?"

She nodded. He glanced her way, his features harsh. "Pull out your computer."

The tracking device. He thought the device might still be on her. Realization spurred her to flip off the seat belt and reach behind her seat. Pulling out her computer, she let the backpack he'd purchased for her at the sporting goods store slip to the floorboard. She tugged the pliant case off the laptop and looked it over. Nothing.

"I don't see anything. What am I looking for?"

"It'll be small, like a round battery but black. Check again."

She switched on the map light and conducted another quick visual examination of the computer's hard exterior. Nothing seemed unusual until she flipped it over and noticed one round foot was larger than the other three. Attached to one of the black feet was a larger black circle. Using her fingernail, she pried the tab loose and held it in her palm.

She stared at the object like it was a black widow crawling across her hand. Then she punched the window button. Frigid air blasted in.

"Wait! Don't throw it out. We can use it."

Her lips parted in surprise. "Are you crazy? How can we use it?"

"Trust me."

She halted. "I'm not sure I should."

For the first time he took his gaze off the road and glanced at her. Lights from the dash highlighted his frowning features. "All

right. I deserved that. But it's too late anyway. They've already found us. Look back."

She turned. Above them on the side of the
mountain she saw only darkness. Then twin
beams of light flashed high above them as a
car took the outside of a curve.

"Oh, no."

"Watch closely. Are there two cars or just
one?"

Twisting for a better position, she fixed
her gaze on the mountain curves they'd just
passed.

"Just one, but it's gaining fast. What do
we do now?"

"Get down off this mountain as quick as
we can."

"Or die trying?"

Cal exhaled. It sounded tight and slightly
frustrated. She had more to say, but they took
a sharp curve and the tail end of the SUV slid
precariously close to the edge of the road. Her
words were lost in a gasp.

Drina gripped the door handle and the con-
sole and didn't breathe again until Cal eased
out of the turn, away from the steep drop-off
leading to the frozen river below. He tapped
the brakes to slow down. Drina looked back.
The lights of the car following them seemed
even closer. She wanted Cal to speed up but

another switchback curve loomed in front of them.

Cal slowed even more. Drina cringed as headlights flashed through their vehicle. The car was right behind them. An engine revved, bringing the other SUV closer still.

Drina turned to face the front. If they were going to be hit, she wanted to see what was ahead of her. She gripped the handle again.

Cal deftly turned into the curve, narrowly avoiding the other driver's attempt to ram the back end of their vehicle. The tail end slid...and slid until Drina was sure they were headed over the edge backward.

Finally, the back wheels caught. Traction pulled them forward and they shot down the hill with the other car close behind. Cal sped up. Another curve loomed ahead.

"Slow down, Cal! We'll never make it!"

Cal pumped the brakes, slowing the car and coming almost to a stop with the front end pointed toward the edge. He eased forward until the vehicle's nose bumped the guardrail. With his gaze locked on the rearview mirror, he spun the wheel in the opposite direction, away from the drop-off.

Drina turned in her seat.

Trying to ignore her white-knuckle grip

and pale features, Cal focused on his task and gave the car a little gas. The wheels caught and moved, nudging the guardrail again and bouncing back…just enough. He hoped it appeared as if they'd slid into the rail and were stuck.

His foot hovered over the gas pedal, ready to gun it. The other SUV came around the curve fast. Seeing them at the side of the road, the driver revved his engine, prepared to ram the tail end of their car and send them over the embankment.

With the SUV headed straight for them, Cal hit the accelerator. Their vehicle jumped forward, toward the side of the mountain, away from the drop-off.

The car behind nicked their corner fender and crashed into the guardrail. Their SUV spun around on the slick road. Drina screamed. Cal rotated the wheel in the direction of the spin. The car swung around once…twice…then slid to a stop against the side of the mountain.

Cal looked over his shoulder. Red taillights disappeared off the side of the road, plunging down the steep drop-off.

He released his breath. His shoulders sagged and for a long moment he leaned against the steering wheel. Then he shifted into Reverse and tried to back out of the ditch. The tires spun, but finally caught, and the car reversed. As they backed up, their headlights flashed on the tire tracks left by the other car.

"Do you think they're dead?"

Cal couldn't spare a glance for Drina. He threw the car into forward gear. "We're not stopping to look."

The four-wheel drive kicked in and they headed down the mountain at a brisk but safe speed.

As they took more curves, Drina continued to look over her shoulder. Finally, she turned back around.

"I think they're alive. I saw lights and movement halfway down the mountain."

Cal shrugged. "That means they'll be coming after us again."

Drina shook her head with a sharp, abrupt movement.

Cal gritted his teeth. "Would you rather I stopped to help the men trying to kill us?"

"No. Of course not. It's just—you seem so…different. So cold."

"This is how I should have been from the beginning. Cold. Impersonal. Professional. Maybe if I had been, I wouldn't have made so many mistakes."

From the corner of his eye, he saw her

shake her head again. "I don't think a professional would have sacrificed the security of the nation for one little life. Maybe you regret saving me, too."

He jerked his gaze from the road to look at her. "No. Not ever. That was the only thing I did right."

Apparently, she had no quick comeback for his sincere comment. She leaned back on the headrest and closed her eyes. Glad for a reprieve from her caustic remarks, Cal focused on the road, and silence reigned within the car. At long last, the mountain curves eased into a straightaway and he was able to speed up.

Drina lifted her head. "Is that a freeway ahead? Are we off the mountain?"

"Yes, it's a main road, a highway. But we're still in the mountains."

Now that they'd left the twists and turns behind, Cal sped toward the highway on-ramp. He slowed to read the signs, then accelerated the way he wanted to go.

Drina glanced his way once…twice. "The sign says the base is the other way."

"I know. This direction leads to Los Angeles and the CIA's main regional office."

"So we're not going to meet your extraction team?"

He nodded. "We are. But I want Carter and his men to think we're headed to safety in Los Angeles. I'm hoping they won't expect us to double back."

He drove in silence a while longer before they came to an off-ramp. Pulling off to the side, he hit a button and rolled down the window. "Still have that tracker?"

Drina opened her hand. "I've been holding it so tight, it'll probably be imprinted on my palm forever."

"Throw it out there." Cal nudged his chin in the direction of a white, snow-covered field.

Sticking her arm outside the window, Drina flicked her wrist and sent the tracker spinning. It disappeared into the darkness.

Cal pulled back onto the road, crossed the overpass and pulled onto the highway headed back the way they'd come. "Now…if they're not waiting for us, we'll be free and clear."

"What do you mean *waiting*?"

"This highway joins the main freeway at the base of this pass. They know we have to come down one side or the other. I hope they follow the tracker to this side…and won't leave someone watching for us at the crossroad at the other side."

"What do you *think* they'll do?"

He shook his head and glanced in her direction. "If it were me, I'd send people to watch both intersections. But they're short one car. Maybe that'll be our saving grace."

The lights of the dash illuminated her full lips and he watched them thin into a hard line.

"Carter and his men already called ahead to have their cronies set up the road blocks. Don't you think they'll have someone watching the Los Angeles connection? That'll leave Carter and friends free to wait for us where we're going."

"We just took the shortest route and made great time. I'm pretty sure we'll beat all of them to the crossroad."

"Well, at least you're covering the bases... now."

The tacked on *now* ground into Cal's senses. Obviously, she was not happy with his revelations about his multiple mistakes. Truthfully, she couldn't be angrier with him than he was with himself.

Gripping the wheel, he clenched his teeth. He deserved to lose his home and everything in it. He should have checked all of her gear, back at the Red Rock tollbooth. He should have realized Carter was smart enough to track the money and the possibility of an escape attempt on his part. But when Cal saw Drina on the shack floor with Whitson's gun pointed at her, something had changed. A switch had flipped. Suddenly, all that mattered was getting her away, out of harm's path.

Cal gripped the steering wheel. Those feelings had only intensified. He'd held her when she sobbed, and laughed when she came back at him with fast quips. He admired her convictions and felt pain when she discussed the loss of her boyfriend. She confused him. Muddled his thinking. Made him yearn for something he wished he'd never lost.

He'd forgotten his duty and nearly got them both killed. Determined to stay awake, he'd even made it through most of the night. But then he'd dozed. Another mistake.

Something had alerted him, maybe the sudden silence of the storm ending.

It was only by God's good grace that they were still alive. The Lord had seen fit to give Cal a second chance. He had no intention of blowing it this time.

They drove the rest of the way through the foothills in silence. The signs of the storm quickly faded. Cal knew from experience that even though the snow had disappeared, the desert's winter nights would be frigid.

They topped a crest. The small town of Tehachapi rested in the corner of the quiet valley, lit by a few lights.

"It looks like a scene from a Christmas card. I wish we could crawl right into it." Drina's wistful tone cut into Cal, deepening his guilt. He accelerated on the straightaway, determined to get her to safety.

The vast, empty stretches of desert appeared in the distance as they rounded a corner. "And then we drive into that, a deep, bottomless black pool."

Drina's words felt like a finger poked into an open wound. Clenching his fingers around the wheel, he said, "Drina, I'd give my own life for you to be safe right now. I'll do whatever it takes to see that happen."

She gave a slow shake of her head. "The problem is, Cal, everything you *can* do might not be enough."

Cal flinched at her lack of confidence. As if to punctuate the biting remark, a red light on the dash flashed and began to beep.

NINE

Cal tried to keep frustration out of his tone. He didn't want to destroy what, if anything, was left of her hope. "One of the tires is losing pressure."

"Do you need to stop?"

"I don't dare. We're coming up on the main intersection. If Carter's people are waiting on the overpass, it will only draw attention to us. We have to get through first."

As they approached the overhead pass, Drina leaned forward, peering through the top of the windshield toward the road above them. As they went under, she turned and scoured the other side.

She searched for a long while. "Nothing. I see nothing. I think you were right. We beat them down the mountain."

She eased back onto her seat but Cal kept his fingers tight on the wheel. As they left the lit overpass behind, the ominous red light blazed in the darkness.

Three beeps echoed across the car again. Drina leaned closer to Cal to see the monitor. The warm scent of pine drifted up to him, cementing his regret and feelings of loss. He tamped down on those emotions and tried to reassure her.

"It's a slow leak. I felt a bump when we spun into the ditch. We probably hit a rock. I'll get us as far away from here as I can before I have to stop."

Cal drove for miles before the beeps echoed again and the monitor read 40 percent. He took the next off-ramp, reduced speed and drove along a frontage road. A white building loomed in the distance.

As they drew closer, the building took the shape of an abandoned gas station. An aging portico extended over old-fashioned gas pumps. The glass-fronted store reflected their headlights as Cal turned in and pulled to a stop in front of the single-car garage.

"Wait a minute." Drina looked around. "We must be close to the base. I think I've been here before."

"Even if you haven't, you've certainly seen it. This is a popular spot for movies and commercials. They change up the look so they can use it over and over again."

He left the car running but turned off the headlights. Crossing to a corner of the building, he found a large rock and used it to break the padlock off the garage door. Then he drove inside and hopped out to pull the large door down again.

Without pausing, he opened the hatch of the SUV. The back end was stacked with weapons and equipment. Carter had enough guns for a small army. At least if they caught up with them again, Cal had plenty of weapons to use. He even found hand grenades like the ones he'd used in his cabin.

Shaking his head against the regret that shot through him, he grabbed the handles of the first duffel bag. "I've got to change this tire. It's going to take a while. You might want to get out and stretch."

Drina slid out but left her parka in the car. Cal tried not to notice how slender and graceful she looked, how she held her arms against her body like she was in pain. "You're going to need your coat. It's freezing even in this building."

His fingers were already feeling the chill. Ignoring him, Drina walked toward the small door leading to the storefront portion of the building. He noted that she rubbed her arms briskly as she walked.

He supposed he deserved her contrariness. Maybe he should have kept silent about his mistakes, waited until he'd gotten her to safety before he revealed his blunders. She might have been more cooperative. But somehow, he couldn't force himself to lie to her again. Not even a lie of omission. Shaking his head, he applied himself to his task.

"Do you think there's a bathroom in there?"

He glanced over. She stood by the door, shivering.

"Probably, but I doubt the water is turned on."

"Too bad for them. I'm going to use it, water or no water."

She hurried back to the car and fiddled with her parka for a few moments. He noted with grim satisfaction that she had her parka on when she headed toward the store.

With the weapons unloaded at last, he found the jack beneath a panel on the floorboard. He placed it under the car and jacked the vehicle high. Then he started on the lug bolts. Three came off easily but the fourth was difficult. He pounded on it, wrenched with both hands and twisted until he was breathing heavy and his hands hurt. He had to rest for a moment and only then realized Drina hadn't returned from the bathroom yet.

He was about to drop the jack handle when he saw her exit from a small door at the opposite end of the store. Picking up the crossed jack handle, he started on the wheel again. The lug nut simply wouldn't budge.

As much as he hated to ask, he needed help. "Drina, come here." Motioning to the wheel, he said, "I'm going to hold this in place with both hands. I need you to stomp on it with your foot. Let's see if we can move it."

He placed the handle and gripped it. Drina stepped on it with most of her weight. Cal barely managed to hold it in place. "Again."

She stomped again and the handle spun out of his hands, painfully banging one of his fingertips. Nursing the injured digit, he picked the handle up, put it in place and started again. He thought he felt the bolt give a little, but the handle slipped loose and landed on the floor with a loud clatter.

Repressing a sigh of pain and frustration, he picked it up once more and Drina stomped on it once, twice. The second time, it fell away again, banging his injured finger in the same place. But this time he was sure the lug gave a little.

Nothing to do but keep at it. He picked

up the handle and fumbled it with his aching finger.

"Great." Drina's voice was heavy with sarcasm. "After all we've been through, we're going to be defeated by a stupid bolt on a wheel."

Cal drew in a breath, biting back his pain and frustration. "It's called a lug nut and it's not going to defeat us."

He placed the handle in position. She raised her foot. "Forgive me," she said, stomping with all her might, "if I no longer have that faith."

Cal gritted his teeth tight before answering, "Drina, I'm sorry. I didn't want anything like this to happen…"

"Please don't say *sorry* again. You can't say that kind of thing one minute and follow your company's risky policies the next."

The lug nut gave way with such force, the handle clattered to the floor, trapping Cal's finger beneath it. Aching from the pain, physical and emotional, he lunged to his feet.

"That's enough."

Drina stepped back and he stepped forward, pinning her against the car. He placed his hands on both sides of her head, trapping her. "I've apologized for my mistakes and paid for them with everything I own. But I'm not going to apologize for my work again."

That soft scent of pine drifted up to him. She looked up, her hazel eyes wide and her lips, so soft and red, he couldn't resist. Leaning even closer, he stooped and covered her mouth with his.

Her lips were cold and soft and so incredibly sweet. To his surprise, she kissed him back, grasping the edges of his jacket and parting her lips. When he would have pulled back, she drew him closer. After a long while he broke away, tilted her chin up and kissed one corner of her mouth, then the other.

He felt her lips tremble beneath his.

Was it the cold? Or was she frightened? He looked down. Tears had pooled in her eyes. All he wanted to do was wrap his arms around her and hold her close.

But he'd lost that privilege. All he had the right to do now was try to save her life.

"I'm sorry." With a sigh, he tugged her fur-lined hood up around her head and ran the back of his finger along her jaw.

Her gaze flickered. "You saved my life twice. I shouldn't be mad at you."

"But you are."

She grabbed his hand and held it to her cheek. "Yes, but I'm not sure why."

"Maybe because I made foolish mistakes. Maybe because you're frightened. Maybe both."

She nodded and rubbed the backs of his fingers against her cheek again. "You swooped in and saved my life like…some superman." Her tone was soft and broken. "I thought… thought you were pretty near perfect and invincible."

Cal felt the loss of her warmth almost instantly, like a part of his own body had been torn away. Still, he stepped away. "I told you not to put your faith in people. The only one who will never fail you is God."

"And I told you. I don't have that kind of faith. But for a moment you had me convinced that impossible things were possible, Cal."

"Impossible things? Is this the point you talked about, Drina? The one where you make a conscious decision to trust or to have faith in me or God?"

She lifted her bleak, unblinking gaze. "I'm talking about impossible things like 'God really cares.' If you were wrong about all those other things, maybe you're wrong about that, too. Maybe He isn't out there, watching over us like you said. Maybe all we really have are our own instincts and judgment."

Her words shocked him. Rocked him where he stood. He stepped even farther back.

"That's your parents talking, Drina, not you. You have faith. I've seen it shining in your eyes…when you talk about John, in the work you did with the poor…even in your deep desire to save the lives of soldiers. You've trusted and let God into your life."

"Yes! And every time I have, He's let me down. First with John and now…"

She didn't finish, but her unspoken words slapped Cal as viciously as a hand.

"It was *my* judgment that was wrong, Drina. My mistakes that got us here. Just because I failed doesn't mean God will fail us. If I'd put aside my own feelings and stopped to pray about my choices, He would have guided me in the right direction. I'm sure of it."

"I'm sorry, Cal. I wish I had that confidence or that faith. But I don't. I have to make my own choices, my own decisions. I'm not going to rely on some invisible, distant force that probably doesn't even exist."

She turned, pushing past with her shoulder as she headed to the front of the car. Climbing in, she slammed the door.

Cal stood, unable to move as his last and worst failure sank deep into his bones and darkened his soul.

* * *

Cal closed the door, then pulled out of the garage, turning the SUV toward the east where gray fingers had begun to thread their way through the black sky. By the time they moved off the frontage road and onto the highway, the gray had begun to turn pink.

Several times Drina felt the urge to look at Cal, to loosen her guard and be honest. Truthfully, she didn't blame him for their situation…at least not as much as he blamed himself. His skills had saved them over and over again. She hadn't forgotten—didn't forget—as he navigated the SUV down the highway, where she didn't know east from west or north from south.

She should have eased his conscience, let him off the hook. But her own disappointment kept her in check. She'd honestly begun to hope there was a happy-ever-after for her. She wanted a life beyond her work but most of all, she wanted to believe God was real, that she was safe in His hands, that her parents were wrong and there was more to life than what one could see and touch. She yearned for the peace that John and Cal's strong faith gave them, a faith that was true and rooted in a loving God who would forgive and take the burden of responsibility off her shoulders.

Once again, she'd been disappointed. There were no perfect men, fairy-tale endings or all-powerful beings to ease her burdens. Her fledgling faith was crushed once more and the disappointment was so keen, she almost pounded the dash in front of her. Instead, she clenched her hands into tight fists. How had she been so foolish…so gullible…again?

She knew now that she could only trust her judgment. That was why she'd turned on her cell phone and called Bill Carlisle from the gas station's tiny, old-fashioned bathroom.

Bill had picked up his phone on the second ring. She was so glad to hear his voice, she almost couldn't answer. When she finally did, Bill told her over and over again how relieved he was to hear from her.

She'd described where they were. Bill recognized their location and said they were only a short way from the base gates. He promised to have troops waiting for them. Guards with guns to protect them from Carter and his men.

She could trust Bill. He would make everything right. Cal had been wrong to suspect her boss. He'd been wrong about a lot of things.

He was no superhero. Just a simple man who loved food and music and cared about people. He cared so deeply, he'd risked his own life for her.

And he loved fun. Even though Cal had failed at the most important things, Drina couldn't forget the things he had done right, like reminding her how to have fun. She'd forgotten how to enjoy life until Cal showed her how. Their time in his cabin was like a dream come true…until Carter and his men destroyed Cal's safe haven. Sorrow washed over her and she closed her eyes.

My feelings are flip-flopping like a fish on shore. We need to reach safety. Once we're safe, I can think clearly, can sort through all these conflicting feelings and disappointments. Right now I have to focus on reaching the gates and handing my computer over to Bill. Then I'll be safe and Cal can stop risking his life to save mine.

Drina's thoughts halted. Was that the real fear driving her? That she might lose Cal like she'd lost John?

The realization broke through her anger and she finally relented and turned to look at him. The pink-and-gray sunrise shed light on his strong profile. Still handsome. Still perfect. Straight nose. High cheekbones. That stubborn lock of black hair falling over his forehead in the same way. The shadow of a beard darkened his chin and hid his dimple. The beard added a rakish, rugged look to his boy-next-door features, features she longed to touch with her fingertips and lips. More than anything she wished she could ease the tightness in his jaw. But she couldn't. She had to face the truth.

It was possible to fall in love in one night. But it wasn't possible for that love to last. Disappointment was sure to follow. Disappointment and disillusionment…with not-so-perfect supermen and a God who only made wispy promises.

Drina faced the road, willing the miles to pass quickly. In the distance and off to the right a cluster of buildings rose out of the shadows, still dim, but growing more distinct as they crossed the miles. The base gate and guardhouse. Safety. All they had to do was take the off-ramp. Safety was just a few miles down that road.

Something metallic flashed on the frontage road. A car…multiple cars, parked on the opposite side of the distant overpass. Black SUVs were parked in a line, just waiting for them to hit the off-ramp.

Carter and his men were waiting to intercept them before they reached the safety of the base. Drina had been so lost in her thoughts, she hadn't even noticed Cal begin to slow. He came to a full stop on the shoulder of the four-lane, divided highway.

Before Drina could even think, he spun the car around and headed back the way they'd come, driving on the wrong side of the highway.

"What are you doing? Are you crazy?"

Cal didn't answer. Behind them, the rising sun sparkled and shimmered on the shiny chrome of a huge semi headed straight for them. The semi honked. Cal gripped the wheel and stepped on the gas.

The semi honked again and Drina pushed on the floor as if she could apply the brakes. "Cal…" Her tone rose as she reflexively stomped at the empty floorboard.

Just ahead was another overpass with ramps. Cal was headed for the on-ramp. He was trying to make it there before the semi…

Cal jammed the accelerator down. The semi hit the horn again, honking loud and hard as the driver began to slow his vehicle. They were only a few feet away from a collision when Cal swerved their SUV onto the ramp and it shot ahead of the passing truck.

Drina heaved a sigh of relief as Cal barreled up the off-ramp, still in the opposite direction of any oncoming traffic. Slamming onto the brakes, he brought the car to a skidding halt. He turned left onto the overpass and Drina sagged.

He was running away, back the way they'd come. Farther away from safety. They were on the run again.

But instead of taking the ramp to the freeway, Cal pulled onto the frontage road. As soon as the road leveled, he jumped over the curb onto the desert floor and immediately turned the car into a spin.

"What are you doing?"

He didn't take the time to answer but drove farther into the desert and began another doughnut spin, kicking dust high into the air. He did it three more times until a huge, dirty cloud filled the sky around them.

Then he bumped back onto another road leading deeper into the desert and a nearby solar farm. The farm covered a two-mile square block of solar panels mounted on poles and tilted toward the morning sun in the east.

More dust billowed into the air as Cal circled again. The dust cloud he'd created completely concealed them. Between the glare of the solar panels and the dust, Drina doubted they were visible to the cars following them.

Cal guided the car up the ramp leading to the fence and locked gates surrounding the solar field. He gunned the gas, ramming the gates. The chain and lock gave way and the gates flew open.

"Do you see Carter and his men?" Cal asked as he deftly handled the wheel on the gravel road.

Row after row of solar panels blocked her view of the freeway and the distant overpass. "No. I can't see anything over the panels."

"Good. Keep watching. Let me know if you can see them or the freeway. If we can see them, then they can see us. I'm trying to throw them off and buy us enough time to reach the base."

Cal kept on the outer back rim of the field, headed the way they'd come. Between each row of panels was a lane wide enough for the SUV to pass through.

As the dust cleared, Drina scoured the freeway for any sign of vehicles following them. She soon spotted Carter's cars, barreling down the freeway, headed in their direction.

"I see them. They're coming this way."

Cal slammed on the brakes, pulling the SUV to a stop at the end of the closest row of solar panels. They were completely hidden from view by the massive panel.

They waited. The car's engine gave off a low hum. At last, a cloud of dust kicked up and traveled down the dirt road that led deeper into the desert.

"They missed us. They're going away!" Drina couldn't contain her excitement.

"For now. It won't take them long to discover we doubled back." He pulled down the narrow row between the panels until they came to the exterior service road. Cal turned onto it and plowed through another locked gate at the far end of the solar field. They bumped onto the frontage road and within moments they were crossing the overpass, headed toward the base gates.

"I can't believe we lost them so easily." Drina spoke softly, almost as if the men following them could hear.

"They won't be far behind us. We just need to get to the guards before they realize their mistake."

Zooming down the two-lane road, headed toward the buildings in the distance, Cal glanced her way.

"The guards may have questions when I show them my ID card. Just let me do the talking. I'll get us through. My team is probably already waiting for us at the rendezvous point. We lost precious time changing that tire."

He glanced her way, expecting a response.

She reached behind and pulled her backpack onto her lap. She ached to tell him about the call she'd made to Bill.

Her emotions must have shown in her features because he said, "Are you all right?"

She nodded again. "Yes. Just anxious to get this over with." Her tone was tight, clipped. She couldn't help it. Lying to Cal didn't feel right. Maybe she should tell him the truth, explain why she'd called.

The moment was lost as Cal slowed to a stop at the gates. A uniformed guard approached the window. Cal pulled his wallet out of his back pocket.

"Morning, sir." The soldier was young. His features set. Was it Drina's imagination or did he look nervous?

Cal handed him the card. The young man nodded. "This isn't your vehicle, Mr. Norwood?"

Cal hesitated. "No. I'm borrowing it from a friend while mine is in the shop. Is there a problem?"

"No, sir. None at all." The young guard glanced up and over the car. Drina followed his gaze, looking to her right, out her window. Another guard stood beside the car with his gun pointed straight at her. She screamed.

Cal's head jerked around. Other guards

hurried out from behind the building and the sides, all pointing their guns at the SUV.

The young guard with Cal's ID still in his grip motioned. "Keep your hands off the steering wheel, sir. Hold them up where we can see them."

Another guard opened Drina's door. "Step out of the car, Ms. Gallagher."

Cal's head jerked in her direction again, surprise written in his features. He quickly recovered and tried to cover his reaction with a calm mien. "Do as he says, Drina. I'm not sure what's going on, but everything will be all right."

"Step out of the car, sir."

Cal obeyed as Drina, clutching her backpack, was led around the front of the vehicle. When they were standing side by side, Bill and a group of men in suits exited the guard shack.

Relief flooded Drina and she ran into Bill's arms. He gripped her tight. "I'm so glad you're safe!"

Drina nodded. "We're both safe. I wouldn't be here now if not for Cal."

She turned back. Surprise had wiped Cal's features clean...just before a frown furrowed his brow and shaped his face into a look

Drina would never forget. It was so full of hurt, Drina cried out.

"No, it's not like that." The soldiers ignored her, still holding their guns pointed at Cal. Desperate, she turned to her mentor. "Did you hear me, Bill? Cal saved my life."

"Of course. Of course. Smith, have those men lower their weapons."

Drina recognized the man beside Bill as part of Cal's security team. Smith signaled to the soldiers. They pulled their rifles back but held them in a ready position and kept a tight semicircle around Cal.

Something wasn't right. Drina looked from Bill to Smith and back to Cal, who stood frozen, his posture slumped and his features slack. Cal acted as if he didn't care what was going on around them...as if he'd lost the battle.

But we've won. We're safe!

Alarm rippled through her. "Tell them to stand back, Bill. We've had enough of guns and threats."

He nodded to Smith, who signaled to the soldiers. Instead of moving back, they pointed Cal in the direction of a blue air force van parked on the other side of the road.

"What's going on?"

Bill wrapped his arm around Drina's shoulders and pulled her in the direction of another van. "Don't worry. We're just moving to a more secure location. We don't want to sort through all this out here in the open."

He led her away.

"I want to go with Cal."

Bill shook his head. "Smith has to conduct his own debriefing. It has nothing to do with you. You can join up with Norwood when it's all done."

Looking back over her shoulder, she saw Smith open the sliding door of the van. Cal climbed in like a man walking in his sleep. Obviously, he felt betrayed, defeated. Her call to Bill was a confirmation that she'd lost all confidence in him.

She didn't mean to betray him but she had to do what she thought was right. She had to trust where logic had led her, had to trust her own judgment. Didn't he see that? Didn't he understand? She needed to talk to him... to explain.

"I want to ride with Cal." She moved forward but her mentor grabbed her elbow.

"Smith has some questions for Cal. He doesn't want you there while he asks them. Trust me. They'll sort this out."

He lifted her into the van and she sagged back against the seat. Bill's words eased her concerns but only a little. She wouldn't feel right until she spoke to Cal.

They drove far from the gates, past the building where she was first kidnapped. The new location was remote, on a rarely used portion of the base called the rocket site. To her right were massive metal stands, built to mount and test rocket engines for the Mercury, Gemini and Apollo projects first initiated by the US government in the race to the moon. The stands had long ago fallen out of use and were abandoned. Now they rusted on a lonely hilltop in mute testimony to a bygone era.

Drina shivered and turned away. "Where are we going?"

"Smith has secured a location for us. It's quiet and safe."

They drove past a work team on the side of the narrow road. To a man, the workers in hard hats and yellow vests stopped and stared as the caravan passed.

"I guess it's not as quiet as you supposed." Drina's discomfort added sarcasm to her tone.

Bill leaned forward and said something to the man next to the driver, who lifted his cell phone and began to text. Bill eased back into his seat, his features calm, collected, as if nothing was amiss.

But something *was* wrong. Drina felt as if she were walking on a bed of rocks, uneven and tricky. Nothing felt right…not from the moment she'd seen Cal's defeated features and they'd ushered him into a van away from her.

Perhaps she'd been on the run so long she'd forgotten how to relax. Or maybe her adventure had taught her to be cautious. She wasn't sure. She only knew her senses were on full alert.

They followed Cal's van to the top of the hill. It pulled around to the back of a cluster of buildings, out of Drina's sight. Her van stopped in the front. The door slid open. A man in a suit helped her down as Bill stepped out and took her arm, leading her inside the older building. It appeared to have been built in the fifties, with low windows and linoleum floors that had seen better days.

Bill escorted her to a back room. Sunshine fell from a mud-streaked window onto a large, old-fashioned metal desk. A rotary phone rested next to a wide paper blotter that had yellowed with time.

"Does that even work?" Drina asked, gesturing to the phone.

"I doubt it. This place has been out of use for a long while. Would you like some coffee or water?" Bill asked as he eased into a chair behind the desk.

She shook her head. "What are we doing here?"

"We're waiting for a signal. Smith hoped the men chasing after you might attempt to follow you onto the base with their fake IDs. The soldiers are waiting to see if any cars matching the description of your kidnappers' vehicle arrives. Of course, we don't want you anywhere near there if they do. You've had enough shock and trauma. Once Harris gives us the all-clear signal, we have a helicopter waiting. Your parents are worried sick. I promised them to get the three of you together as soon as possible."

"My parents? You contacted my parents?"

"Of course, Drina. You've been missing for days now. We had to contact them."

His tone sounded so concerned, so solicitous. It should have warmed her. But it didn't.

"Is that your computer you're clutching so tightly?"

She nodded.

"Set it down. Try to relax."

Biting her lower lip, she eased her bag onto the desk. The man behind her pushed a chair forward. The legs squeaked across the linoleum like fingernails on a chalkboard. The sound sharpened Drina's senses, awakened something dead inside her. Two thoughts jumped into her mind.

First, Bill had a helicopter at his disposal. Maybe like the one that had chased them through the wind farm?

Second, Bill said the guards at the gate were waiting for vehicles that would match the description of the vehicles chasing them.

But he never *asked* her for a description.

Why? Because Bill already knew what the vehicles looked like?

Cold washed through her. She started to tremble. Linking her fingers together, she gripped them to hold them still. Cal had been right all along. Bill was the boss.

TEN

Drina looked at the man she had called a friend and mentor. He was watching her with a direct, piercing gaze.

"Is everything all right?"

Swallowing hard, she nodded. "I think maybe shock is setting in. I think I *would* like a cup of coffee."

He gestured to the man behind her but didn't move from his chair. She'd hoped he'd get up, leave her alone for a moment so she could gather her thoughts.

She had to get away, out from beneath his all-too-knowing gaze. "I need to use the restroom. Is there a bathroom in this building?"

He gestured to the door. "To the left. It's at the end of the hall. We'll have that coffee for you when you get back."

She stood on shaky legs and almost tripped as she moved from the office. An exit door framed the end of the hallway. An old-fashioned bathroom sign extended from the wall, marking the entrance. As she walked toward it, she glanced through the glass top of each office door, searching inside for someone… anyone. All she found were more abandoned desks.

Where was Cal? Was he in a different building?

By the time she reached the bathroom, her legs were so shaky she couldn't stand. She opened the door, stumbled into the cold and fell against a row of dirty white sinks, holding herself up with sheer effort.

The bathroom smelled old and so foul she gagged. Suddenly, she was gasping, heaving with full-blown panic. She needed air. Needed to breathe…and think…and find Cal.

Above the stained sinks was a row of clouded windows, all closed and locked. Drina climbed on top of a sink to reach the latches. They were stuck tight with disuse and age, but she finally managed to pull one up and slide the window open. Leaning forward, she dragged the cold, crisp air into her lungs.

After a few deep breaths, she opened her eyes…just in time to see Cal, his hands bound behind his back. Carter stood behind him, using the butt of a gun to shove Cal into the back of his black SUV.

Drina gasped and almost cried out. Pressing her fingertips to her mouth, she stifled her cries as Carter hit the back of Cal's bowed head. He slumped over the back passenger seat. Carter shoved the rest of his body into the vehicle, slammed the door and walked around to the driver's side. Then he sped off, leaving a trail of gravel and dust.

Hot tears spurted from Drina's eyes and flowed over her hands, still pressed tightly to her lips. She slid off the sink and collapsed to the floor.

All the pieces suddenly fit together. Bill's piercing gaze as he studied her, wondering if she suspected. His calm, calculated tone. He lied so easily. Fooled her so completely… for years.

Bill was the leader Cal had been so earnestly trying to expose. From the beginning he'd suspected Bill and worked to keep Drina safe from him. Now she had betrayed the man who had saved her life time and again, handed him over to a man who would kill him at his first opportunity.

Drina sobbed into her hands, trying to stifle her cries from her captors. There was nothing she could do. She was trapped as completely as Cal. She couldn't help him any more than she could help herself. Bill had no intention of sending her home. She doubted she would even leave the base alive now that he had her computer.

Fresh tears racked her body and she shook with fear. She'd been such a fool, so very, very wrong. Cal had been right…about everything.

Please, Lord, forgive me.

Her thoughts came to a stumbling halt.

Had she just prayed?

Of course she had. And it wasn't the first time. Memories of prayers tumbled through her mind. When she'd waited for Cal on the hill, she'd prayed the quad would start. At the cabin, she'd prayed that Cal would be waiting for her by the vehicles when she emerged from the snow-filled gully. Those were just a few of the times she'd silently turned to God. Now that she realized it, she could remember countless other times when she had unconsciously sought God's comfort and help. Not just in the desperate times since her kidnapping but for years.

Cal had been wrong about one thing. He'd told her faith was a lot like falling in love. *Make a conscious choice and let it happen. Once your mind makes the choice, your heart will follow.*

But in her case, her heart had made the

choice a long time ago. Her mind and stubborn will just refused to follow.

Well, that time was over.

Biting her lower lip, she closed her eyes and whispered, "Lord, please help me. I've been so wrong about You, about trusting my own judgment over Yours. I know I was wrong, but please, please, don't let Cal suffer for my mistakes. Help me find a way to help him. I don't care what happens to me, just don't let him die. He deserves more. Please, Lord…"

Her whispered words broke into sobs and she sagged against the gritty, filthy floor. She felt as dirty as the broken tiles.

Cal opened his eyes slowly. Sharp, shooting pain made him close them again. He heard a voice growling into a phone.

Carter.

"I don't care what you say. This whole thing has fallen apart and Norwood killed my partner. No way am I gonna let him live… and he's gonna suffer before he dies."

The harsh, strident rumble of another voice sounded clearly over the phone.

"Yeah, well, you go ahead and take off without me. I'll find my own way out of here."

Cal opened his eyes just in time to see Carter throw his phone across the front seat.

The car swerved around a sharp corner and Cal rolled onto the back of his head. He bit back a groan as he touched the spot where Carter hit him.

Although, why should he bother to control his response? It was over. He'd lost. Everything he feared had come to pass and he was about to die. Drina had betrayed him. She didn't trust him. She'd turned her back on her fledgling faith and placed her trust in a man who wanted to kill her—*would* kill her—and there was nothing Cal could do to stop it.

From the sounds of it, Carlisle had his helicopter waiting. He'd spirit Drina to someplace where no one would ever find her, and when Carlisle was finished with her, she'd disappear. Just like what was about to happen to him.

The vehicle swerved again. Cal rolled forward and used the movement to test the handcuffs on his wrists. Tight. Painfully tight. Sticky moisture indicated he might have cut himself on the zip tie edge of one wrist.

Carter was taking no chances. The man was determined to see Cal dead. This side trip wasn't about business. It was vengeance.

Funny. Drina had accused him of acting out of vengeance. Maybe she was right. Maybe if he hadn't been so determined to stop Carlisle and Carter, Drina would be safe and maybe, just maybe, he would have survived.

Now he was going to die.

The car hit a bump. Carter was speeding. A foolish action. Military police were notorious for their strict speed limits. Carter was sure to garner attention.

The thought jolted the fog in Cal's pain-filled mind.

Garner attention. His extraction team would be on the alert for any unusual activity. If he could create something...

He lay with his head directly behind Carter. His legs—stretched across to the passenger side of the vehicle—were free. If he could twist enough, he might be able to kick at Carter and distract him.

He might also cause him to crash the vehicle.

What difference did it make? He was going to die anyway. Better to die fighting.

Lord, forgive me for getting offtrack. For losing focus on You and You alone. Please don't let Drina die for my mistakes. Help me in my hour of need. Don't let me fail again.

Taking a deep breath, he bent his knees, one slow, silent inch at a time. Then with one quick movement, he lunged and spun. One leg caught on the passenger seat. He used the momentum to push his other leg higher and rolled.

He connected with something. With his face buried on the seat, he couldn't tell what. But Carter cursed. The car jerked and spun around, once…twice…again. Cal was flung sideways. His head hit the door and everything went black.

Drina lay on the floor. Cal's words floated back to her. *He poured out His life for us. He poured Himself into a cup of salvation. All we have to do is accept that cup.*

"I do accept. I do," she whispered.

Another cold, clear revelation pierced her as she lay on the filthy floor.

Two incredible, wonderful men—two amazing men of God—had loved her. She had been blessed. God had His hand in her life all along. He could—He would—show her the way now.

She sat up and wiped the tears from her cheeks with both hands.

There had to be some way out. What could she do?

Nothing. She was trapped, caught in Bill's web. He had her work…

Her thoughts coalesced. Bill was after her work. Her equations. She would not—could not—let him have them. She would destroy her computer before she would let him make use of the sensitive and dangerous information it held.

Gripping the edge of the closest sink, she pulled herself up. Her legs shook and wobbled. She gave herself a moment to breathe, to recoup. Then with determination flowing through her limbs, she quietly opened the door.

One of Bill's men stood in the door of the office where Bill waited for her return. "Boss, Smith wants to talk to you outside."

Bill started out of the room. Drina ducked back inside the bathroom and pushed the door almost shut, careful to make no sound. Soon, Bill's footsteps crossed the crackling old linoleum. She peeked out as the guard opened the front door and followed him outside. Drina caught a quick glance of Smith waiting for Bill before the door swung shut behind them.

Whatever Drina was going to do, she had to do it now, before Bill returned. She eased out of the bathroom and hurried down the hall, moving as quietly and quickly as possible.

Her backpack rested on the desk where she'd left it. She shoved it over one shoulder and hurried back down the hall. She made it to the back door without being caught and pushed on the handle.

Locked. *Now what?*

The bathroom windows. Hurrying back into the cold, smelly room, she crawled on top of the sinks and slid the window open as wide as it would go. The opening was narrow but still large enough for her to slide through.

Gripping the backpack, she used the hard computer to break through the old-style metal screen. She pierced a center hole, peeled back the metal edges and folded them as flat as she could over the sill. Then she dropped the backpack on the ground outside.

Thankful for the protection of her parka against the sharp edges, she slid through the narrow opening. She tried to swing her feet free so they would drop first but the window was high enough off the ground that she still toppled over backward and hit the ground with a bone-jarring thud.

She held her breath. Had anyone heard her ungraceful landing? When no guards came around the corner, she rose to her feet and ran straight back, using the building as a giant shield to stay out of their view for as long as possible.

The direct path behind the building led her up the hill to the platform of abandoned test stands. She'd almost reached the top when she heard a cry. Someone had finally spotted her!

Don't stop and don't look back.

Cal's words flashed through her mind. Pumping her legs as fast as they would go, she ran across the large, weed-filled cement area. The test stands were poised on the edge of the hill maybe a quarter of a mile away. The ever-present Mojave wind whistled across the mile-wide platform, rattling the stands into a creaky response.

A block building with a large metal door stood at the base of the closest test stand. Drina ran for it. Behind her, shouts filled the air, and car engines ground to life.

She grasped the door handle of the block building and jerked, pulling with all her might.

Locked.

What now? Her gaze raked the area around the platform. The cliffs. She ran to the edge, hoping she could climb down and cross the dry lake bed that served as a landing strip for the base. Surely someone would see her crossing the wide, prohibited area and alert the authorities.

Years of testing rocket-engine propellant had changed the cliff. Heat and flames had roared down the side of the hill, melting the rock into one continuous, slick slide of at least four hundred feet. No way could Drina climb down without tumbling to the bottom.

Her gaze raked the platform for some sort of shelter, some other way to go. The only other escape route was up. A metal ladder attached to one leg of the nearby test stand was accessible. Puffing and panting, Drina ran across the pad, nearly tripping on tufts of weeds and grass sprouting out of the broken cement.

She couldn't quite reach the bottom rung, but an empty metal box rested nearby. She shoved it under the ladder, climbed on top and grasped the bottom rung. She'd managed to get one ankle over the rung and pulled herself up to the next when the blue air force van came into view, barreling and bouncing over the hill.

Taking a deep breath, Drina reached for the next rung and climbed. Rung by rung, she hurried up the windy, rattling test stand.

A rusty rung screeched and spun in place. Drina almost lost her grip. Her feet slipped, banging her shins against the ladder.

Groaning against the pain, she struggled to regain her footing and clung to the ladder for one breathless moment. The wind gusted through, whipping her hair and stealing her breath. The entire test stand shook like an earthquake had hit.

Was the metal behemoth swaying? Would the whole rusty tower topple over the side with her added weight?

She clung to the ladder, wishing she could climb back down or at the very least, stay where she was, but the sound of approaching vehicles spurred her to move. Reaching for the next rung, she continued her upward journey. If she could get high enough, someone from the main base might see her. If nothing else, she'd drop her computer over the edge and destroy it. She might have to follow it down but one way or another, Bill was not going to get the information.

The stand was built on levels. Metal girders crossed from corner to corner and marked the first level. Drina reached the first girder and stepped to the side to catch her breath.

"Drina, don't be a fool. Come down."

Ignoring Bill, she reached for the ladder and continued to climb. The rung she grabbed spun and screeched. Rust fell loose in her hands, loosening her grip again. She slipped and almost fell. Someone screamed.

Latching onto the side of the ladder, Drina clung to it and looked down. Her mother stood beside Bill's SUV, and her father was climbing out of the back seat.

"Drina, please!" her mother called out "Stop this nonsense and come down. What do you think you're doing?"

Her mother's tone was the same condescending tenor she'd used to reprimand Drina when she was younger. That tone always had the power to make her feel foolish and silly.

But not this time.

"Mother, what are you doing here? Don't you know…"

"I've told them how your kidnapper has influenced your thinking, Drina," Bill called. Was it her imagination or did he sound like he was laughing beneath his words?

Her mother stepped forward. "Drina, I'm trying to understand what you're doing. Whatever that man told you isn't true. Please, dear. Please come down. Bill isn't going to hurt you."

Drina couldn't remember a single time her mother had ever called her *dear*. It was a sign of her stressed state.

"Listen to your mother, Drina." Her father's voice, so calm, so logical. "I don't know what that man did to you, but you're not thinking clearly. Come down so we can sort through this."

Not thinking clearly, Drina closed her eyes

and leaned her forehead against the railing. Of course they would believe she was the problem. Even now, while she was running for her life, her parents didn't trust her judgment. All these years they'd had her convinced they were so perfect, so right, so... invincible.

As the wind whipped around her and chilled her to the bone, another thought hit her...froze her to the ladder and made her legs tremble until she wavered and almost lost her grip.

Was that why she was so hard on Cal, so disappointed in him? Did she think she'd met the perfect invincible partner to carry her through life? Someone who would meet and exceed her parents' expectations where she had failed so many times?

The truth hit Drina hard, and she caught her breath in a gasp. It was true. She believed she'd found the perfect man.

What she'd really found was the man perfect for her. Cal was a good man, capable and incredible, but he was not a superman strong enough to stand up to her parents...parents who stood below her, clueless to the danger they were in because there was no way Bill would let them go free now.

She'd been wrong to put such faith in her

parents—in any human. Cal was right. God was the only One strong enough, loving enough, to never fail her. She needed to put her faith in Him. He would guide her.

"Please, Lord, help me. Show me the way." Her whispered words were torn away by the wind.

Somehow she found the strength to loosen her grip, to reach for the next rung on the ladder.

"Don't think I won't have my men shoot, Drina," Bill shouted. "I will."

Glancing over her shoulder, she looked down. One of Bill's goons had pulled her mother away from her father and placed his gun against her temple.

"What are you doing? Let her go!" Her father took a step toward the man and Drina cried out.

Smoothly, without even pausing, the man aimed his gun at her father's heart.

"Stop! Don't shoot!" Drina slid the backpack off one shoulder then the other. Looping her elbow through the ladder, she leaned out as far as she dared and held the backpack out from the side of the test stand, directly over the slick rocks and steep drop-off.

"If you hurt them, Bill, I'll drop it."

"Drina, you know I don't *want* to hurt

them. Come down. I'm sure we can work this out. All I want is the computer."

He sounded so calm, so reasonable. Like the man she had thought she knew. She wanted to believe him, wanted to give in to the familiar tones she'd trusted for so long. But he was also the cunning leader who had eluded Cal for years. The man who had ruthlessly ordered her death. If she listened to him, neither she nor her parents would survive.

She shook the backpack over the drop-off. "Let them go, Bill. Now!"

Bill paused, indecision in his stillness. He didn't believe her, didn't think the Drina he knew, the Drina driven by work, would let go of her life's accomplishment.

He didn't know the new Drina, the newborn child of God, ready and willing to do His bidding. She leaned out farther and allowed the backpack to slip down her arm to her fingertips, where it dangled precariously.

With an abrupt, frustrated movement, Bill gestured to his man. The goon lowered his gun and stepped away from her mother. Her father hurried forward and wrapped his arm around her waist.

"Mom, Dad, go!"

"Drina…" Her mother hesitated, reached

for Drina, but her father wisely pulled her away. Drina watched them turn and walk toward the back of the SUV. When they were clear of the vehicle, her father grasped her mother's hand and ran down the road. Drina watched them until Bill motioned his men up the ladder after her.

Now what?

Drina would never be able to fight those men off once they reached her level. They'd take her backpack and push her off the stand. She leaned into the ladder and closed her eyes.

Stifling a cry that sounded almost like a sob, she reached for the next rung and began to climb higher, stalling for time. Rung after rung, higher and higher. The wind tore at her parka and stung her eyes, making each step more difficult.

She didn't know how high she could climb or how long she could evade them. She only knew she had to keep trying. Her muscles ached and her hands burned from abrasions caused by the rusty metal. She was growing tired and weak and the wind seemed determined to rip her off the stand.

Over the whistling wind, she heard more cars. Drina paused and looked down. A military police jeep sped over the crest of the hill and bounced down the road. Another jeep followed, trailed by multiple SUVs and vans.

Cal! He must have escaped from Carter and alerted the CIA. It had to be Cal coming to her rescue…again.

Drina cried out and waved so hard she almost lost her footing.

Below, Bill and his men also saw the approaching cars. The men dashed for their vehicle. The ones following her hurried back down the ladder, now desperate to reach the ground. The driver started the engine but Bill stood still. One of the men who had been climbing the test stand reached the ground and ran by his boss. Bill stopped the man long enough to grab the gun out of his holster.

Lifting it, he took careful aim at Drina.

"I've wasted too many years on you. You're not going to win."

Drina cringed. She clung to the ladder, expecting a bullet to pierce her body at any minute. Bill's first shot whizzed over her head and pinged off the metal stand.

She looked down. He was aiming again. One of his men ran from the car and grabbed his arm.

"Boss…we gotta go. Leave her."

Bill shoved the man away, but the man wrestled the gun down and pushed Bill toward the car. Even before the door closed, the vehicle screeched away, heading across the test stand pad at a high speed.

Drina sagged against the ladder. Drained and weak, she clung to it as one of the SUVs in the caravan pulled to a stop beneath her.

Wind whipped over her, rattling the stand with its eerie breath. Only then did Drina find the strength to start climbing down. Weeping happy tears of relief, she practically fell into the arms of the military policeman waiting at the base of the ladder. The stout soldier half carried, half dragged her toward the cars. He held her upright. Balancing on wobbly legs, she looked around.

"Cal? Where's Cal?"

The man who exited the car whipped off his dark glasses. "That's what we were hoping you could tell *us*, Ms. Gallagher."

"Cal's not with you? I was certain he escaped... Wait... Who are you?"

"Agent Harris, ma'am. I'm with the CIA."

She clutched Harris's jacket. "You... We have to find Cal. Carter will kill him."

Harris motioned an agent behind them forward. "Can you give us a description of the vehicle?"

She closed her eyes, trying to remember details. "Carter knocked Cal out. Pushed him in the back seat of a black SUV and drove away. I'm almost a hundred percent certain it was Carter's car, the one we left at the base gate. Carter must have been right behind us, waiting for Bill to take us away so he could retrieve his vehicle."

She shook her head, frustrated with Bill's duplicity and her own gullibility. "I should have known…should have listened to Cal."

"Can you give us more info about the car?" Harris prompted.

"I don't remember a license plate. I spent most of my time inside it, not out. But I do know the make and model."

She told them, and another agent lifted a radio to repeat her description. She racked her brain trying to remember some identifying mark.

An image flowed behind her closed eyes. She saw the interior of the SUV as they hurtled down the mountainside, the electronic dash lit up with lights and the view out the window…

"Carter's car had all kinds of electronic equipment, so much it needed two antennae. It had two antennae on the right side of the hood!"

Harris nodded. "We'll find him. I promise." He turned to his men. "I want eyes in the sky now, and alert the guards at all the gates. Those men are not leaving this base."

One of the military police said, "Sir, we have housing not far away. Civilians and schools. We could have a chase-and-hostage situation."

Nodding, Harris said, "Inform the commander. Put lookouts on all roads leading into the housing. My guess is Carlisle and Carter will head away from populated areas, deeper into the desert." He stared into the distance for a long moment. "Someone get me that map of the base."

An agent hurried to the car. A man came from another vehicle and handed Harris a headset. He put it on and stepped away to talk.

Drina stood silent, clutching the straps of her backpack and shivering. Harris glanced over while speaking. When he finished, he walked back to Drina. "Your parents have been taken to a safe location. I'll have one of my men escort you to them."

She shook her head. "I'm not going anywhere. Not until we find Cal."

"Ms. Gallagher…"

"Let's not waste time arguing, Agent Harris. I'm not going."

A wry smile flitted over his lips. "Cal said you were a brave, quick-thinking woman."

A trickle of warmth flowed through the ice in her veins. "Cal said that?"

"Well, actually he might not have used the word *woman*. I think *challenge* was his exact term."

She nodded. "He was right. I can be a challenge. So you know you won't convince me to stay behind. Besides, I might be able to help."

"How?"

She nudged her chin in the direction Bill's escape vehicle had taken. "If Bill and his men get off this hill, they'll be heading for a helicopter. He said he had one waiting."

"Do you think he was just trying to throw you off?"

"No. He has a helicopter at his disposal. One chased Cal and me through the wind farm."

Harris gestured to the last military policeman standing by. He'd sent all the others scurrying with duties to perform. "Contact the flight line. See if they have any helicopter takeoffs scheduled."

When the officer had gone, Harris said, "The minute I called for the search, all flights should have been delayed. That holdover might buy us some time. We'll find him."

He nodded, almost as if to reassure himself as well as Drina.

"If Cal didn't alert you, how did you know I was up here?" she asked.

"We've been searching the area ever since we lost Cal's beacon in his safe house. The military police alerted us to some unusual activities at the guard shack, and travel through this whole area was closed for road-work. When your caravan of vehicles showed up, the workers called the MPs to complain. Since you and Cal had missed your rendez-vous time, we were already on high alert. We knew something was wrong."

She took a deep breath. "That something was me. I didn't believe Cal's suspicions. I called Bill and told him to meet us."

A man stepped out of the SUV. "We have a helicopter already in the sky. It spotted a vehicle traveling east at a high speed."

"Does it have two antennae?"

The man put the phone back to his ear before nodding. "Confirmed."

"Get the coordinates." Harris gestured to the back seat of his SUV. "Ms. Gallagher, let's go get our man."

Drina climbed into the back seat, where she was sandwiched between two agents. As they sped down the rocket site road, the driver plugged coordinates into the GPS. A man beside her pulled out a paper map and compared it to the GPS coordinates.

"There's a service road just ahead, sir. It cuts across the desert. It'll save us several miles."

"Contact the helicopter. Tell them not to make a move until we're in place." Harris turned back to her. "Buckle up, Ms. Gallagher. The road is going to get bumpy."

Drina followed his instructions, her heart in her throat. Cal had said almost the same thing to her when she'd climbed onto the back of the ATV at the wind farm. It seemed appropriate somehow that she'd come full circle.

She also remembered Carter's cold, calculating moves that day when it all began. He was ruthless then, and now he was desperate. He would do anything…including wreck his own vehicle or shoot Cal for spite.

ELEVEN

Cal had been bouncing around the back seat like a rag doll for miles. He was groggy from the second knock to his head, and blood trickled from his nose...probably from a blow Carter had administered while he was unconscious.

His last ditch effort to stop the man had failed. He didn't have the inclination to fight anymore, and doubted he could find the strength anyway. He drifted in and out of semiconsciousness.

After what seemed a long while, he roused to a steady buzz. Close. Annoying. It seemed to be everywhere. It took him some time before he recognized the hum of a helicopter.

So Carlisle hadn't abandoned Carter after all. Anytime now he'd stop the vehicle and it would be over.

The car shot right, making a sharp turn, and bounced high as it went off the pavement.

They hit another bump that knocked Cal into the air. He bounced back down with a grunt.

Still, Carter never slowed. Several times the vehicle felt like it was airborne, until finally the car shot upward then dived straight down into a ditch. Something wasn't right. Carter wouldn't have risked that breakneck pace if Carlisle was above them.

The helicopter hovered. Dust filled the air and clouded visibility. Cal coughed and tried to rise. Carter shoved open his door. Before Cal could get up, the other man had grasped his arm and yanked him out. He could barely stand. Even as he wove back and forth, the cold tip of a gun pressed against his temple.

He heard running feet and tried to focus enough to see beyond the dust cloud. Had he recognized one of the voices?

Finally, the dust cleared. Agent Harris and several other agents ran toward them. They skidded to a halt as they saw the gun at Cal's head.

"That's right," Carter yelled. "Stop right there if you want your boy here to stay alive."

"If he dies…" Harris's tone sounded low and dangerous.

"It'll be your fault," Carter called back. "Now, tell that helicopter to set down somewhere close by. It's going to give me and my friend here—" he gave Cal a vicious jerk "—a ride. And tell Ms. Gallagher to step out of the vehicle. She and her precious computer are going with us."

"Don't move, Ms. Gallagher," Harris called to Drina without turning his head.

Drina? Drina was in the car. Every inflamed nerve ending in Cal's body came to attention. The sudden surge caused his knees to buckle and he dipped forward. Carter's grip tightened on Cal's neck. The choke hold gagged him, but his thoughts galvanized.

Drina was alive and safe…unless Carter got his hands on her again.

No way was Cal going to let that happen.

Harris had ordered Drina to stay in the car as his men piled out. For the first time in a long time, she obeyed. Too tense to sit still, she gripped her backpack and scooted to the edge of the seat.

When the dust cleared and Carter appeared outside the car, holding a gun to Cal's temple, she gasped and clutched the bag tighter. Blood ran down Cal's face and neck. His hair was thick with it and he wove back and forth in a groggy manner.

"I wouldn't stall for too long. Norwood's

not too steady on his feet. I can't be held accountable for my actions if he drops."

As soon as the words left Carter's lips, Drina understood the truth. Cal was dead even if Carter got his way. The madman had no intention of letting Cal live.

But if she turned herself over, bargained for Cal's life, maybe...just maybe... Moving deftly, Drina unzipped the backpack and let her computer slip to the floor.

After zipping the bag again, she scooted across the seat, never taking her gaze off the scene in front of her. The minute she opened the door and stepped out of the car, Carter's gaze jerked in her direction. All of the men turned, their gazes jumping between her and Carter.

"Ms. Gallagher..."

"It's all right, Agent Harris. You and I both know he's not going to let Cal live."

Carter's lips stretched into something that was supposed to be a smile. Drina had never seen anything more evil. "Well, you'll never know unless you come along, Ms. Gallagher." He drew the *Ms.* out trying to sound sarcastic. He succeeded in sounding menacing as well, but it was precisely that menacing, nasty tone that hardened Drina's resolve.

"Oh, yes, I will, Carter. Because Cal's not getting on that helicopter with us."

Carter's smile faded. "I'm calling the shots here. You don't tell me what's going to happen."

"If you want this—" she held up the backpack "—you'll do as I say. Release Cal. Let him go, and I'll climb on board with your boss's money as an added bonus."

Cal's knees buckled again. Carter jerked him back, shoving the gun closer to his temple while his gaze darted from Harris to Drina. He hesitated so long, Drina was sure he was plotting a new move.

"Make up your mind, Carter. Me and the money or Cal. It's up to you."

He was silent for a long while, the black barrel pressing against Cal's temple.

"All right. Deal. Come forward."

"No way," Harris called out. "She's not getting anywhere near you. All you have to do is drop Cal with one shot and grab her."

"Then what do you propose, Mr. Agent Man? A polite exchange over a bridge?"

Harris was silent for two beats. "I'm coming with Ms. Gallagher, my gun trained on you. You drop Cal, I drop you. End of stand-off."

Carter's expression broadcast what he

thought about Harris's suggestion. For a moment Drina was certain he'd decided it wasn't worth the risk. She held her breath, fearing Carter would kill Cal and shoot it out with the other agents.

Then his expression changed. He nodded. "It's a deal. Both of you come ahead. The girl first."

Harris hesitated, then nodded and motioned to Drina. Cal's knees dipped again. He fell forward, with his head slumped, but raised it just enough for Drina to see the steel blue resolve in his gaze.

She caught her breath again as he sagged forward. Carter jerked him back, but this time, Cal found his balance. As Carter pulled, Cal's head jerked back in one swift, lethal move, connecting hard with his captor's nose.

Carter's head bobbed. Blood spurted and his gun dropped. Cal flung his body even farther back, knocking Carter off balance and pinning him against the vehicle. With agility no one suspected, Cal thrust his shoulder upward into Carter's chin. The man's head bounced against the SUV with a thud.

By the time he slumped to the ground, the other agents were beside Cal, knocking Carter's gun away and pinning him on the ground with his arms behind him.

Drina ran to Cal. Harris had already turned him around to cut the zip tie binding his wrists. Before he was even loose, Drina had her arms around him, pinning his arms to his sides, so tight he couldn't move.

"Oh, Cal, I thought I'd lost you."

He pressed his lips to the top of her head. "I wasn't sure you *wanted* to find me," he murmured.

Drina squeezed him tighter. "I did, Cal. Of course I did." She leaned back to search his face. "You were right...so right about everything. Bill. Accepting the cup of salvation and God's plans. Even falling in love in one night. Especially that. I did fall in love... I mean I do—"

Cal had managed to wiggle his arms loose during her breathless explanation. Cupping her face with both hands, he kissed her, silencing her rambling sentences. The kiss was tender and oh-so-thorough before he lifted his head and traced his thumb over her lips.

"All you had to say was *I do*," he whispered.

Then he kissed her again.

Drina wiped the fogged mirror in the hospital bathroom with her towel. The hot shower had eased her aching muscles but still, every part of her body hurt.

The last time she'd hurt this much had been in Cal's cabin. The memory made her cringe. His beautiful home, his LP collection, everything in his cabin had been destroyed. It was a hurt she couldn't quite get over. She couldn't imagine how Cal must be feeling.

After the agents secured Carter, EMTs had arrived. Harris ordered them to transport Cal and Drina to the hospital for examinations. Cal had a concussion. Drina had suffered multiple cuts and bruises, as well as dehydration. The doctors decided to keep both of them overnight for observation.

The last Drina had seen of Cal, he was being wheeled away on a gurney. They'd pumped her full of fluids and she suspected something to help her sleep, because she'd not woken until this morning, sore and sluggish…but glad to be alive.

Determined to find Cal, she'd hopped in the shower then searched the closet and all the cabinets in the room for her clothes. All she found was her parka and tennis shoes.

Someone from the kitchen staff entered, carrying a breakfast tray.

"Excuse me… Where are my clothes?"

The young woman shook her head. "Sorry,

ma'am. I work in the kitchen, not here on the ward."

The tray gave off a wonderful scent. Scrambled eggs, oatmeal and a cinnamon-spiced roll. Drina's stomach growled and put up such a fuss, she was forced to crawl back into her bed and accept the tray.

A few more minutes won't matter.

She dug into the eggs, finished off the oatmeal with sips of orange juice and savored every bite of the cinnamon roll. The food went a long way toward easing the ache she hadn't even noticed in her tummy. The hospital's fare didn't even begin to compare to the food Cal had prepared, but it did the job.

She rang the buzzer for the nurse and eased back on her pillow, feeling every cut and bruise. Maybe the doctors were right. It might be a good idea to take things slowly today. She closed her eyes for just a moment and didn't open them again until Agent Harris entered.

"I thought you might like these." He held up a clothing store bag. "Your old ones were a little worse for wear. But we used the sizes to get you some new stuff."

Drina found a pair of jeans, underwear and a long sleeved red T shirt in the bag. "These are for me?"

Harris shrugged. "Like I said, it's the least we can do."

Drina murmured her thanks and pulled the items out for a closer look.

"I thought you might also be interested to know Carlisle and his men were arrested as they attempted to board a helicopter at the Mojave Airport. He's in custody, and undergoing a cross-examination as we speak. I think it's safe to say his black market ring has been destroyed."

Drina breathed a sigh of relief. "That's wonderful. Cal managed to salvage his work after all."

Harris frowned. "I'd say he had a little help from a very brave young lady."

"A little *help*? I almost got us killed when I contacted Bill. Mostly I just got in the way. Cal saved my life time and again."

"You'll have to tell him that. He seems to consider this mission a failure. I've offered him a very important post in Washington, but he's considering leaving the agency."

Drina stared at Harris. "He can't do that! We need men like him, godly men, willing to stand for what's right, for everything that's good and just. We need…" She almost said *supermen*. But caught herself just in time. She looked up to see Harris smiling.

"Something tells me you might be able to change his mind. Speaking of positions, we haven't been able to determine how deeply Carlisle penetrated your company."

"What do you mean? Is my company under investigation?"

"Apparently Hal Jacobi has been collecting data on Carlisle for some time. He felt he didn't have enough real evidence to support his suspicions and besides, he thought the security team leader, Cal, was working with Carlisle. We're talking to Jacobi now, comparing notes to determine how many of your company's projects might have been compromised."

"Do I still have a job?"

"It's hard to say. Time will tell. Until then, you're a guest of the US Government. It's the least we can offer after you risked your life to protect us."

"And my computer?"

"I'm holding it safe until you know where you're going and what you want."

"Thanks, Agent Harris. That puts my mind at ease."

"My pleasure, Ms. Gallagher." He turned to leave but paused. "You know, the CIA has a very interesting research and development department. We could use a shrewd, quick-thinking challenger…if you're interested." A smile hovered over his lips. "That is…when you decide where your future is going."

Drina smiled, too. Harris and all his agents had witnessed Cal's kiss. She knew exactly what he was implying.

"Your parents are anxiously waiting outside. I told them I needed to debrief you. They were…very concerned." His careful tone told Drina there was more to their interview than he was saying. If she knew her parents, they'd probably hit Harris with more accusations than concerns.

Drina sighed. What would they say if she told them she was considering a job with the CIA? Even worse, a romantic future with an agent?

At least she hoped she had a future with Cal. They hadn't spoken since that last breathless kiss in the desert. She'd tried to call him in his room but hospital personnel wouldn't give her the number. But that was a matter for later. Right now she had to deal with her parents.

"I understand. I'm ready to see them."

Harris gave her a quick salute then opened the door. Her mother hurried inside, looking weary and more frazzled than Drina had ever seen her. She rushed across the room and threw her arms around Drina before she could even call out a greeting.

"Oh, my dear."

Dear again. Obviously, her mother was still stressed.

"We're so glad you're safe. When I saw you leaning away from that ladder... I... I..." Tears filled her eyes and she hugged Drina again.

"Mom." Drina felt tears forming in her own eyes. "It's over now. I'm safe... We're all safe."

"Yes. We're all safe...thanks to your quick thinking. I've never seen anyone act so quickly or courageously."

Her father's sincerity brought more tears to her eyes. She ducked her head. "That's because you've never met Cal Norwood. If you had, you'd know I was just following in his footsteps."

"Agent Harris speaks very highly of the man." Her father's tone was approving.

"I can't wait to meet him and thank him." Her mother gripped her hand. "If anything had happened to you, Drina..."

Drina didn't quite know how to handle this new, emotional side of her mom. She hesitated, but just for a moment before she decided to do what seemed natural. She leaned forward and pulled her mother in for a tight hug.

"I can't wait, either, Mom. He's very special," she murmured.

They exchanged a quiet look, and a smile flitted over her mother's lips.

"Well, I for one will be very glad to get on a plane and put all of this behind us." Her father sounded flustered, out of his element.

Drina sighed. "I'm not sure I'll be going back with you."

"What do you mean, not going back?" Now her father sounded even more flustered.

"I'm not sure what's in my future, Dad. I'll have to wait and see. Besides, Agent Harris says I might not have a job to go back to. In fact, he's offered me a position with the CIA."

"The CIA? They almost got you killed. Surely…"

Her mother placed a calming hand on her father's arm.

"Whatever you decide will be fine with us, Drina. You know what you're doing."

The softly spoken words silenced Drina's father and filled Drina with unexpected pleasure.

"Thanks, Mom."

Her father cleared his throat. "Of course

you do. Of course. We'll support whatever decision you make."

It was tough for her father to step out of control mode, but Drina appreciated his effort.

"We've booked a suite at a hotel. We'll be staying here for a while. Is that all right?"

Drina smiled. "Yes. It's more than all right. That'll be wonderful."

"Good. Why don't you get dressed, and we'll check you out of the hospital."

"First I have to find Cal and talk to him."

"We'll wait in the lobby."

Her mother tugged her father out of the room. He still seemed to be floundering in unfamiliar territory, and his unaccustomed awkwardness made Drina smile. He needed a good shake-up because there were many changes ahead of them.

Determined to find Cal, she climbed out of the tall hospital bed and pulled on her new jeans and T-shirt. She'd just removed the tags from her new socks and was slipping into her shoes when someone knocked.

"Come in."

Cal stood in the doorway. He wore new clothes, too—jeans and another of the waist-hugging, long-sleeved T-shirts he seemed to favor. He looked healthy and strong, except for the white bandage across his forehead and that one stubborn dark curl that curved against the white patch.

Relief surged through Drina and she hurried toward him, her shoelaces flopping on the tile.

Wrapping her arms around his slender waist, she said, "At last. I was beginning to think something was wrong. I tried to see you, but they wouldn't tell me where you were."

Cal allowed her to hug him for a moment before he grasped her arms and gently eased her back. "I know. I asked them to keep you away."

"What...?" Drina's question came out in a whisper. "You didn't want to see me?"

"Of course I did. But I thought... I thought you needed a little space, some time apart, time to think."

"To think...about what?"

"Drina, the kind of experience we just went through...sometimes danger like that can mess with your mind. Shock and fear can make you think and feel things that aren't real."

Drina stepped back. "Not real?" She shook her head. "When I saw Carter pushing you into his car... I fell apart...fell to my knees. I begged the Lord to help me, to save you. He answered my prayers, Cal. Peace filled me. That was the most *real* experience of my life."

She stepped forward and placed her palms flat on his chest. His heart pounded against her fingertips. "I've placed my life in His hands, right beside yours. I can't wait to learn more, to see where He takes us."

Cal's handsome features were unreadable, and her thoughts clouded with despair. "Unless…are you telling me you don't feel the same way?"

He grasped her hands. "Not a chance, Drina Gallagher. You said, 'I do.' I'm not letting you get away without trying to make that true."

Drina smiled. "Are you sure? They tell me I'm a challenge. I don't follow protocols. I don't even *know* the rules."

His lips lifted in one corner with the wry twist Drina had come to love. Sliding strong, capable hands over her hips, he pulled her closer. "I'm sure I'm the right man to further your education. We covered music. I think we'll move on to the cinema."

Curling her fingers around his neck, she pulled his lips close to hers. "Good. Let's start with *Superman*."

* * * * *

If you liked this book,
try these other danger-filled
Love Inspired Suspense stories:

DEEP WATERS
by Jessica R. Patch
HIGH DESERT HIDEAWAY
by Jenna Night
WILDERNESS REUNION
by Elizabeth Goddard
DEAD RUN
by Jodie Bailey

Available now from
Love Inspired Suspense!

Find more great reads at
www.LoveInspired.com

Dear Reader,

I have a funny story to tell about *Mojave Rescue*. My husband was an electronic warfare engineer. So you can see where I got my inspiration for Drina's occupation. Many years ago he took me on a tour of the air force base where the rocket stands are located. They were in disuse and rusting and very spooky. I thought it would be a great location for a mystery. My husband agreed and said he would be glad to help me with details.

It took me six months to come up with a story I thought would work...about top secret plans for a satellite that would orbit the earth and shoot down any missiles coming into US air space. I even had a great name for it... *Star Wars*.

I enthusiastically told my idea to my husband and asked his advice. He promptly told me the idea wouldn't work and he couldn't help me. In fact, he didn't think I should write the story. Frustrated and confused, I dropped the idea. Two weeks later the paper announced that the president had signed a bill to fund a new program called Star Wars where a satellite would shoot down missiles. They had renovated the rocket site test stands and my husband had been videotaping those tests for the previous month. If I had written that story, no one would have believed that I came up with the idea on my own and his job would have been in jeopardy!

My husband is retired now. We sold our home in the Mojave and have moved into a motor home to travel. With his career behind him, I felt safe enough to create a new story set in the Mojave. Many aspects are different but one detail is the same…that eerie place on the hill called the rocket site. It seems appropriate that my first story with Love Inspired Suspense should be set in the place I called home for over thirty years.

Tanya Stowe

Get 2 Free Books,
Plus 2 Free Gifts—
just for trying the Reader Service!

Love Inspired®

Get 2 Free Books,
Plus 2 Free Gifts—
just for trying the Reader Service!

YES! Please send me **The Hometown Hearts Collection** in Larger Print. This collection begins with 3 FREE books and 2 FREE gifts in the first shipment. Along with my 3 free books, I'll also get the next 4 books from the Hometown Hearts Collection, in LARGER PRINT, which I may either return and owe nothing, or keep for the low price of $4.99 U.S./ $5.89 CDN each plus $2.99 for shipping and handling per shipment*. If I decide to continue, about once a month for 8 months I will get 6 or 7 more books, but will only need to pay for 4. That means 2 or 3 books in every shipment will be FREE! If I decide to keep the entire collection, I'll have paid for only 32 books because 19 books are FREE! I understand that accepting the 3 free books and gifts places me under no obligation to buy anything. I can always return a shipment and cancel at any time. My free books and gifts are mine to keep no matter what I decide.

262 HCN 3432 462 HCN 3432

Name	(PLEASE PRINT)	
Address		Apt. #
City	State/Prov.	Zip/Postal Code

Signature (if under 18, a parent or guardian must sign)

Mail to the **Reader Service:**

IN U.S.A.: P.O. Box 1867, Buffalo, NY. 14240-1867
IN CANADA: P.O. Box 609, Fort Erie, Ontario L2A 5X3

* Terms and prices subject to change without notice. Prices do not include applicable taxes. Sales tax applicable in NY. Canadian residents will be charged applicable taxes. This offer is limited to one order per household. All orders subject to approval. Credit or debit balances in a customer's account(s) may be offset by any other outstanding balance owed by or to the customer. Please allow 4 to 6 weeks for delivery. Offer available while quantities last. Offer not available to Quebec residents.